To CATHE

OLLIE SAVAGE
By
RICHARD MAUTO
Instagram & Twitter
@richardmauto

i

CONTENTS

PREFACE iii

ACKNOWLEDGEMENTS iv

CHAPTER ONE 1

CHAPTER TWO 9

CHAPTER THREE 14

CHAPTER FOUR...23

CHAPTER FIVE 37

CHAPTER SIX...47

CHAPTER SEVEN 55

CHAPTER EIGHT 68

CHAPTER NINE..86

CHAPTER TEN..93

CHAPTER ELEVEN..98

CHAPTER TWELVE 106

CHAPTER THIRTEEN 112

CHAPTER FOURTEEN 120

CHAPTER FIFTEEN 152

CHAPTER SIXTEEN...160

CHAPTER SEVENTEEN 167

CHAPTER EIGHTEEN..174

CHAPTER NINETEEN..193

CHAPTER TWENTY 205

THE END..212

PREFACE

This novel is based on real life experiences. It has been repeatedly described as 'emotionally draining'. However emotional readers may find it, please be reminded that it was created for entertainment purposes only.

ACKNOWLEDGEMENTS

I would like to thank my supportive family for putting up with me during the writing of this book. We have done it team Mauto, thank you all.

CHAPTER ONE

Ollie looked and sounded English. Had you met and spoken to him; you'd never have guessed otherwise. However, he was as African as they come. Born and raised in a remote Zambanian village, he had outgrown his own expectations by becoming one of the brightest criminal masterminds of modern Britain.

His women saw a brilliant lover, his children saw an amazing father, his neighbours saw a smart businessman on the come up. To his inner circle of gangsters, he was an exceptional leader and problem solver, but underneath all that facade was a conflicted man, constantly seeking approval and acceptance. You could sum up that Ollie surely was a sexy beast.

Ollie was in too deep by the time he realised how he was passionately focused on anarchy and chaos. Stuck in the oblivion of a failing asylum system, he felt his best years were being stolen from him. The perpetrators? 'The system'. Whatever they stole from him for all those years, he would stop at nothing to get it all back. The odds of getting refugee status in Great Britain are not in his favour, but he wouldn't care less once he got his way.

Ollie was a class A student in his rural village's day school, but that did not stop him from dreaming of a much bigger life. As a sweet and innocent choir boy in his early life, he had never stolen even a teaspoon of sugar. He had never dreamt of the life he found himself in. His childhood dream was to become a doctor, so he could cure his mother's long suffering with hypertension. A dream he only shared with his endearing girlfriend, Yinka.

OLLIE SAVAGE

Ollie and Yinka had grown up together, and had a bond only shared by husband and wife, since childhood. Seeing them innocently holding hands whenever they met, Yinka's grandparents saw it fit that they treated young Ollie as their future son in law. Whenever the guardians met, they couldn't help but fantasize about their young ones getting married one day. In this remote village, planning an arranged marriage at this early stage is the norm.

There are no career prospects here, they simply send their children to the free government schools to equip them with basic education. There is no pressure to get good grades or to go to college let alone university. These children are simply the first generation to attend modern education: maths, English, geography etc. The only crucial education most of their parents or guardians ever received was how to sign X on official documents.

As Ollie and Yinka come along together, they grow a likeness for one another that they cannot yet explain. As they play their childish games, they do not play the roles of siblings but those of a married couple. Their imaginary children are told, "give this to your father or say this to your mother." They make promises to each other that, if ever one should go to the city for work, they should come back and get the other out of the poverty that besiege their village. They have come a long way and have overcome too many obstacles such as famine and diseases to get here.

As secondary education wraps up, it is the last day of attendance. Ordinary level certificates are being handed out and the young adults celebrate their greatest achievements. Now aged sixteen, most of these young men will not make it out of the village.

OLLIE SAVAGE

As a lucky few get out to find work opportunities in the capital city, Chekwa, those who stay behind will apply to their village chiefs for a piece of land. They will get a pair of young oxen, a young cow and any other livestock from their fathers as they begin their transition into adulthood. The system here is simple yet sufficient. It teaches them responsibility and indigenisation.

As far as tradition goes, the night of high school graduation is a special night, marked by an incredibly special celebration. Ollie and Yinka had long decided they would not be passing up on the long tradition. As they celebrate their biggest achievements thus far, Ollie and Yinka lay bare on a pile of soft hay, under the shimmering light of the full moon. Yinka has finally submitted herself to her first love, Ollie.

The young teens have finally fulfilled their promise to lose their innocents to one another. As Ollie dismounted from the comforts of Yinka's warm body, he hailed a deep sigh of distress. This worries her, it is not what she expected from him. A traditional thank you would have been adequate, after giving him the honour to pave her way into womanhood.

He had a reason; something was eating at the core of his soul. He had not been totally honest with her. Had he told her the truth, perhaps this special night would have been a missed opportunity. He is only here to say his goodbyes. He will be leaving for Chekwa, at the break of dawn. He has a ticket with him, for a direct flight to London tomorrow morning.

With his "O" level certificate, passport and flight ticket in hand, he leaves the village life, his family and the soon to be expecting first love behind him. While enjoying the flight and the hospitality within, England seemed only ten minutes away, not the ten hours he has been on the actual flight.

He got off the plane before he had fully savoured this wonderful experience of flight. Not only has he never left the village before, but this has also been his first flight and first solo trip out of the village. For a boy who was born and raised in a village, England was the promised land he had read about many times over in his favourite parable.

He had other reasons for not wanting to land too soon, planes full of UK deportees were landing at Chekwa International Airport every day. This opportunity was too big to miss. The continuous thud in his chest was a reminder of what was at stake here. The immigration officer in front of him could not be more intimidating. At 5 ft 11, sixteen-year-old Ollie was the tallest man in his village, not this Goliath of a man in front of him.

The immigration officer is not happy with something. There is a lot of frustration in his voice and facial expressions. He soon asks him to grab his belongings and wait in an isolated area. He cannot help but hear the other migrants whispering the same worry he has on his mind.

He is sure this is the area where they are sat while sorting out their deportation papers. Thirty minutes later, the officer returns and asks him to follow him back to his desk. Poor communication had led to him being set aside in the waiting area while they fetched his sister Gloria, who was waiting for him in the arrivals' hall.

It worked to his favour that he was an unaccompanied sixteen-year-old kid, in a foreign country, at night on Christmas eve. He is relieved to learn that he has been given the green light, when his sister comes over smiling and telling him they are going home.

OLLIE SAVAGE

Everything about London is different, it is so cold that the sub-Saharan winters seem pathetic. There is heavy snow everywhere and has been like this since November. These English people are so excited about their white Christmas so much that it quickly rubs off on him too.

Usually, he'd be in bed by now, but this is not any usual occasion, he is a Londoner now, as he is thrown straight into the deep end. On Christmas eve, these Bermondsey Londoners have a party at one of their friends' house in Elephant & Castle. He gets showered, dressed and is off into the car.

It is evident, as he meets and greets with other attendees, that they are only just turning up. His sister had not told anyone about his arrival, so he is the big surprise for this flourishing Zambanian community.

He is introduced to all these cousins he never knew he had. These people call each other brothers and sisters and are tightly packed, just like back in his village. He cannot help but wonder which girls are safe to hit on, if all the girls are his cousins. Talk about killing his vibe.

There are these identical twins he really fancies, but unlike him, they have not bought into this cousin nonsense. One of them whisks him away and starts a conversation with him. She starts off by calling him sexy and handsome as she compliments him. He blushes and asks to go back inside. He cannot believe how this new cousin is already committing an abomination, less than ten minutes into knowing her.

Sexy is not how you'd refer to your cousin back home. She quickly realises her mistake, and she tells him to stay put while she fetches him some smokes and beer. This is now leading somewhere, beer it is. A few Stella Artois cans later, and in his head, he speaks fluent English.

5

OLLIE SAVAGE

The next afternoon, he wakes up to some booming music and the heavenly smell of west African food his sister is preparing while her husband, the self-proclaimed Dj Skee, is perfecting his craft on the decks. They are both so relieved to see him back on his feet. Both his nephews jump straight into his broken English quotes from last night. They all laugh intensely at the kids' mimics of him that they cry with laughter.

He laughs it off, but deep down he is embarrassed at how badly he handled the new girlfriend, Stella Artois. Brunch is served, allowing for very little catch up time, as preparations are underway to receive guests for their Christmas party. At least, there is another opportunity to see that cousin whose name he cannot remember. All memories from last night were wiped out, thanks to some unique alcohol handling.

The guests start arriving at around nine in the evening. To avoid last night's repeat, he is only sipping off some of his sister's Lambrini tonight. He is saving himself for the cousin. When she finally arrives, she has brought a date. He still manages to get his shot with her, only to find she is cross with him.

She had caught him jack hammering the only white girl that had gate crashed the party, in the flats' staircase. Funny enough, it was his nephews who had called her to the scene. He apologises and joins Dj Skee at the turn tables, where he stays sober for the remainder of the night.

It's not a good start to the new year, his visa has just expired. He had only been granted two weeks entry clearance, not the standard six months visitors' visa. When he finally gets his sister's attention and tells her about his expired visa, she quickly dismisses his worries and reassures him she will soon get a lawyer and apply for an extension.

Time does not wait; it's already February and the birthday boy is packing up for relocation. He is going to live with his cousin in St Albans, where he can get some help renewing his visa. There is also plenty of male company there, so he will soon learn the ropes.

He gets picked up from the train station, he can't help but notice the major differences between this small town and the big city. This small town is less intimidating, unlike London, there is some type of serenity here. This is village life as he knows it, only with better infrastructure.

It is not long before he starts regular agency work at an amusement park. He works the grill, where he flips burgers in the hot and smoky kitchen. It is too busy, especially during lunch time, but he loves the pressure and the food once he finally takes a lunch break.

The manager soon recognises his true potential, and she delegates him with other fitting tasks. He starts switching up between the kitchen and the ice cream stands. The ice cream stands soon start to pay him better dividends. He sells the ice creams in cash, so voiding the correct sells puts all that money in his pocket.

There is no auditing system in place here, except his own recording system. It goes on for almost another eight weeks before he finally gets found out. His girlfriend and manager Sarah, confronts him, but he blatantly denies any wrongdoing. Sarah is disappointed in his dishonesty and she escalates it with the right officials. He was not going to walk into a trap or a surprise arrest, so he saved the day when he failed to show up for the scheduled hearing.

OLLIE SAVAGE

When Ollie is not working on weekends, he is socialising with his fellow countrymen. He enjoys the party life in London, where his brother-in-law Dj Skee is hired to play at private parties and in local clubs where he gets regular work. He gets to play while Dj Skee prepares his set or during breaks.

This puts the spotlight on him and with the spotlight comes all sorts of opportunities. Being the tall, handsome and well amassed young man that he is, Ollie gets approached by women, beautiful women with money and status. Life is going very well for this single young man.

This deejay hustle is only for the spotlight but very little money. He works hard during the week, sometimes working from one job to the next, to meet the demands of the glamorous life he portrays. He has always had a thing for music, he still believes he could be a musician one day. Every once in a while, he finds a hot instrumental and pens some lyrics to complement the beat.

At this early stage, he does not have the confidence to perform his music to the party or club audience. So, he simply plays it to the unsuspecting crowds to evaluate their response. The young thugs seem to lean towards it, but there still is room for improvement.

CHAPTER TWO

This night life is only a diversion, it is a break from the realities of his own life. He gets to be someone other than himself, and what a joy that brings him. He is aware of the responsibilities that awaits him outside of his social life, but for now, those can wait.

Ollie is busy creating a playlist for a very special party. It's an 80th birthday party for a former Nigerian president who now resides in London. Dj Skee got the contract to play it but is not well due to a car accident injury that has left him stretched out on a hospital bed. It was a close encounter with death. His wife and children managed to escape with minor scratches and bruises, while he took the full hit from a motorbike at a T-junction.

He has downloaded a lot of tracks onto his laptop and is playing them one by one, to ensure there are no broken or unexpected jerks in the sound. He reckons, when the stakes are this high, everything must be perfect. One of the contacts he met in a club in Stratford has provided transport and is helping him to pack the heavy equipment into the car. This preparation has given these two young men time to catch up and get to know one another.

"Ay, Ollie, were you born Ollie or that's a pet name?"

"Pet what?"

"Pet name, it's like a street or short name."

"Oh, yeah. "It's a pet name. How do you know all these fancy words man?"

"Books my man, I read a lot of novels."

"You, you can read a whole novel?"

"Yeah."

"I could never get past the first two pages man; I just see through all the bullshit."

9

"It depends on the genre; I like crime thrillers. What genre do you like?"

"I don't like reading; my mind just shuts off and I end up falling asleep."

"Seriously, you should read man. It will improve your English, significantly."

"Damn, if I can sound half as good as you, I will definitely start reading."

"I will get you some of the books that I have already finished reading. There is nothing more dangerous than a gangster that can read, Ollie."

"Oh, about that, I never caught your name man. I have been too embarrassed to ask, I still have your number saved as Stratford Guy," they both laugh.

"My name is Caster, as in the caster sugar."

"Bad motherfucker, no mother calls their son that shit."

"Yeah, it was my father. He was an aspiring baker."

"Was, what happened to him?"

"He chose food over us, he died though."

"Sorry man."

"It's all good, I never really knew the guy," as he looks saddened by the memory of his father.

"Right, I was named Oliver at birth, but my ex, Sarah, called me Ollie. It's an English thing."

"How so?"

"Apparently, I reminded her of some soap character called Ollie. She just never stopped, and I liked it."

"Yeah, was she white?"

"Yeah, my first."

"Oh shit, you gave your innocence to a white girl?"

"No, my first white girlfriend, dummy! She was hot."

"Yeah, did you fuck her?"

"All the time, white girls are freaks, man. She was older, and she liked taking cocaine before we fucked."

"Shit, did you ever take it too?"

"Nah, but she would rub some on her pussy making it all tingly and shit."

"Shit, you fucked my type of bitch."

"What, you like that shit?"

"Well, my bitch is Jamaican. We just smoke some weed and fuck all day."

"I know man, once bitches get high, they don't have none of that shy shit."

"So, where is Sarah now?"

"Oh, we broke up. She had called the cops on me."

"Why, what happened?"

"You'll laugh."

"Try me."

"I was working for her through an employment agency. She was my boss and she caught me stealing money from the ice cream stands. The next thing I know, she arranged a meeting where the police would come to arrest me. So, I bounced."

"Shit, for real?"

"For real, white people are just too honest, man."

"But why did you bounce, did they have evidence?"

"Just receipts from all the voids, but the police wouldn't care. They would have just handed me over to the Home Office, and I'd get my ass deported."

"No Ollie, it doesn't work like that.

"They would have needed evidence like, video evidence to charge you."

"Nah man, the risk was way too high.

"I've learned to just avoid the police, period."

"Why, aren't your papers straight?"

"Nah, still working on them. There is this English lawyer holding my passport for years now, and he wants more money on every turn."

"You need money?"

"Why, you own a bank?"

"Nah, but we can help each other if you need money."

"Sure, I need money, why else would I be playing master and servant with my brother-in-law?"

"Word?"

"Listen, this man is exploiting me man; I only get drinks and bitches from all the work I do."

"Is this your full-time job then, taking scraps," they both laugh.

"Nah, I work through an agency. Sometimes stacking shelves and sometimes working on farms harvesting fruits and veg, hard work man."

"Tough shit, sure sounds like slavery."

"What about you Cas, what's your life story?"

"Not sure about a life story but, I work for myself."

"Doing what at your age?"

"Mainly banking."

"That doesn't say much."

"I find people with a bank account; I deposit money into their account, and we split the money fifty-fifty."

"Word? Where do you get the money from?"

"Just find me the people and I will show you."

"What about me, what's my cut from the fifty-fifty?"

"If you get your own contacts, we can go forty-forty-twenty. All day long."

"Man, with the people I meet every time I play, are you sure you can deliver?"

"All day, every day."

"What about cops, how do you avoid them?"

"Cops never catch anyone, Ollie.

"Their training doesn't cover what we do."

"We, so you work with other people?"

"Not really, tight circle.

"Let's just say, it's a family business."

"Man! So, I am out here slaving off for three hundred and fifty quid per night, when you make how much?"

"Just think thirty to forty grand, split forty-forty-twenty."

"Man, I can retire after three jobs."

"Nah, once you've tasted that level of success, you can't get enough of it.

"Your life changes, your spending changes, it comes and goes too quickly, you will need to keep on hustling."

"Shit! How do you spend yours?"

"All white parties, bubbly, bitches, whips, style, you name it."

"Damn! Now it all makes sense.

"I have always wondered how all these young boys could afford all those fancy cars man."

"Get your hustle on gangster!"

CHAPTER THREE

They soon arrive at the party and Ollie sets up his deejay station on a well-lit stage. The laser lights flash on the vacant dance floor and a master of ceremony will be collaborating with Ollie. As the guests start to arrive, they are scanned by the heavy security assigned to the former president.

Ollie is dressed to impress in a silk white shirt and chequered grey smart pants, complemented by black and white brogues and a black cravat. The long sleeves of his shirt nicely wrap around his defined big arms, shoulders and chest. His pants are skin-tight, clearly showing the definitions of his calves, thighs and ass. This is his signature look, one that gets the ladies drooling over him.

As the party starts, the now frail former president is sat with his first lady, son and three daughters. Around them, is his security detail in civilian clothing, tightly guarding him. More people arrive but the volume is handled by a very tight sitting arrangement. This was by special invitation only.

Ollie feels highly favoured to be playing at this prestigious event. This is as high as he can go as a disc jockey, rubbing shoulders with presidents. He takes every opportunity to hand out the business cards he has printed. From here on, he wishes to play his own parties, the payment he receives here is all he needs to finally pay off the instalments for his own deejay kit.

The party is plain sailing with the deejay software Ollie is playing from. The music plays from the playlist while he fools the crowd with the decks. This is not cheating; this is simply new-era deejaying. The decks are for graphics, some people still want to see the deejay break a sweat. Not Ollie, he is not that type of deejay.

14

OLLIE SAVAGE

The party is coming to an end and the appointed personnel collect parcels and gifts from the seated attendees, who seem as if they are being held hostage. The master of ceremony has spent the night mainly reading out random birthday messages from the sitting crowd. This is a different type of party, which leaves Ollie wondering, where is the fun in all of this, rich folk?

Caster has been cleared by the security and awaits Ollie to come out. They load up his gear and are off to Caster's house. Ollie is allocated a room in the mansion belonging to his mother, a retired doctor now residing in Zambani. The house is one of the few properties she owns that her oldest son Goldie, manages.

A repeated knock on his door wakes him up, the wall clock is stuck on six, but the daylight tells him otherwise. Whoever knocked still awaits a response. He sits up in the bed, with his upper torso uncovered, and asks them to come in.

"Hi, are you Ollie?" asks the tall and slender girl in braces. He covers up a bit more as he is not sure this girl is old enough to be gawking at his chest.
"Hi to you too, young lady.
"Yes, I am Ollie who wants to know."
"I am Caster's sister, Nancy.
"He has asked me to wake you up.
"He will be back soon, to drop you off.
"I have brought you some towels, soaps and creams," she smiles and walks out before he could say thank you, leaving the door ajar.
Ollie doesn't pay too much attention to her as he gets out of bed only dressed in his boxers and socks. As he opens the

curtains and starts stretching, he turns around, only to bump into her.

"I'm so sorry, he wants you to call him from this burner," she leaves him shocked and covering his junk with both hands. He believes this was a set up. "Kids these days," he exclaims.

Caster soon arrives and finds Ollie presented with a meal worthy of a king. Nancy has warmed up leftovers from last night's dinner for Ollie. Caster washes his hands and joins him as they share the brunch.

"Man, I left you with my sister for two minutes, why is she playing house with you all of a sudden?"

"What, she never does this?"

"Never, she hates people. I stopped bringing friends here because she'd hate cleaning after them."

"Friends huh, is that what we are now?"

"Yeah man, we're cool.

"You can pass through here, any time.

"Like really, you should come here often.

"I could get used to eating like this."

"I never thought of myself as the arranged marriage type, but I will think about it," he shouts out loud making sure Nancy catches it.

"I will kill your ass; she is just a kid.

"Don't let that height fool you."

"Ay, I know man, I would never even look at her like that.

"Your sister is my sister too man."

"Good!"

Caster was just being polite. He had never brought guys to his house again, after one of his older brother's friends made unsettling remarks about his baby sister. These boys are very protective of their sister. They don't want her to get teen pregnancy as their two other sisters.

Caster refuses to take fuel money from Ollie, on the way to drop him off. All he wants is for Ollie to find him customers. If he really wants to hang around with these London boys, he has to work just as hard and make some money for himself.

Seeing where Ollie lives, Caster doubts that Ollie can ever make money deejaying in this white populated neighbourhood. He offers him a room to rent in one of their properties in Camberwell, London. At sixty quid a week, it's affordable, as long as Ollie can keep his hustle on.

The icing on the cake is, Ollie can stay close to Caster and learn to navigate these London streets, if he ever wants to make it big out here. It's a deal Ollie cannot resist, as Caster emphasises that there are more willing customers for their banking hustle in London. Approachable people, people who are just trying to make it too in life.

By the end of the month, Ollie has saved up enough money and moved into his new place. It's a big lounge converted into a bedroom, sitting on the second floor. It comes with two sliding glass-doors leading to the street-facing balcony, only he has access to.

He is back in London, where it all began. He gets a job in a fast-food restaurant, where the work is light and he enjoys the food and music. It's a relaxed environment, where he gets to interact with customers and learn their London accent. He reads the novels Caster recommends and he develops a neck for the crime thrillers too, especially where the bad guys win.

Slowly but gradually, he starts picking up on fancy words. His friendship with Caster is solid, however, he does not want in on the cake Caster is bringing in. He lets him have the fifty-fifty splits as he would rather work and earn his money.

He thinks Caster's money is haram and is not different from any other blood money. Receiving a share of it does not sit well on his conscience. Caster takes him to all the fancy clubs in and outside London, introducing him to the high life he is missing out on.

He enjoys the music and Gogo dancing with the ladies, but never alcohol and smokes. He stopped drinking after it foiled his chances with his 'twin cousin', back when he first arrived in England. That led him into believing, alcohol was his undoing.

Ollie and Caster are on the prowl for some nice Zambanian women of marriage material. Where else to get marriage material women than in church, wonders Ollie. They have a list of popular African churches in London. A pattern emerges, as they go down their list, they have been beaten to it.

Most of the church girls are already taken, or the pastors simply won't allow outsiders jumping the queue and taking all their good women. They are shocked at the level of corruption in these churches. Nevertheless, they do not give up, they stick to their mission. Every Sunday they suit up and turn up.

At the burger joint Ollie has been working, the manager has received a letter from the head office, which he presents to him. Ollie's national insurance has bounced back, it does not match with any of the records held by the DWP.

Until he provides them with a valid NI, they will continue to withhold his wages. Ollie is in a panic but remains calm, he calls Caster and shares the news with him. Caster soon picks him up and takes him back to London's Westend, where he was conducting business. Caster can't help his curiosity. So; he asks a few questions to get things straight.

"How did you get your NI Ollie?"

"I got all my paperwork from this one lawyer.

"My cousin and I paid him a ton of money.

"He had my passport for some time, remember, I told you."

"Nah Ollie, look, that shit does not come from no lawyers man.

"That shit comes directly from the DWP."

"Who the fuck is this DWP that everyone knows about, and I don't?"

"Look, chill man. "I've got you! The DWP is a branch of the government called the department of work and pensions. They are the ones who issue anyone from the age of sixteen who is eligible to work here, with national insurance numbers. It sounds to me like you got duped. Just saying"

"Duped, by an English lawyer, with a straight up office?

"Highly doubtful man.

"If it was some African guy with an accent, perhaps.

"Just saying," as he checks Caster.

"I'm just saying man, if it looks like fraud, and it sounds like fraud, it might just be fraud.

"Do you know where this guy's office is, maybe he can explain to us? I say we pay him a visit."

"Nah, I never met the guy myself. He was dealing with my cousin, directly. "I was just the new kid on the block man, I had literally just come over here."

"What visa did he get you?"

"Some green sticker that says indefinite something."

"Indefinite leave to remain?"

"Yeah, that one."

"Good, I've got one of those.

"We can compare to see if there are the same, ok?"

"Whatever man. Just get me some fat booty tonight.

"Link me up with your Jamaicans."

"Yeah, most definitely.

"What visa did you have before that?"

"What's with the thousand questions man, are you with the police or something?"

"Look, I am on your side here, I'm just trying to figure this thing out, just like you bro."

"Look, I came here back in '99, and overstayed for a minute. My sister and her broke-ass couldn't help me out. So, I went to live with my cousin in St Albans, he was the only one who had a bit of money at the time. He is the one who knew this immigration lawyer. He was using the same lawyer for his whole family. He swore he was legit."

"Where is your cousin now?"

"He got deported, I heard there was a problem with his passport when he was returning from Zambani."

"Deported? You see! if he had used the same lawyer, who might have been dodgy, don't you think maybe that's why he got deported? "Don't you think it's possible he was deported for a fake visa?"

"Yeah, I know man, but this shit right here, is just fucking up my Chi."

"Chi, are you sure that's a word?"

"Yeah man, look it up."

"Ok, spell it out for me."

"Chi, as in Tai Chi."

"Never heard of that either, which books have you been reading?"

"Negro please! Are you telling me, you have never watched any Jet Li movies?"

"Nah man, I only watch black movies."

"Then how do you know he is not black?"

"You said, Jet Li. His name sounds Chinese."

"Then you're the most racist black person I know. "Drop me off here, I cannot be seen with a fucking racist."

"Come on Ollie, school me on this. "Let me watch some of your Tai Chi movies then."

"Alright then, remind me when we get back to my ends.

"I have plenty of pirate DVDs."

"Ends, you're too much, Ollie.

"Listen to you, sounding all English already."

"Well, I have been learning from garage music and movies like, Kidulthood. Them kids are sick. I have watched that movie like fifty times already, just learning the dialogue."

"Dialogue? Ok! I liked the trailer, but I'm still to watch it."

"Well, you need to watch it asap, these kids these days, man. "You need to see that shit."

"I will, but when it comes to garage, I'm all about Kano right now.

"Hear this," as he bumps to 'Ps & Qs' by Kano.

"Man, I swear down, Kano isn't garage. "He has that new sound, like Dizzee.

"They are calling it, 'grime'.

"The last real garage was So Solid Crew man."

"Yeah, I agree.

"These new boys sound criminal.

"What kind of genre is grime, anyway?"

"One that rhymes with crime," they both laugh as they leave the car.

Caster has created the distraction Ollie needed. The next day, he does not show up for work. It's time to move on and find another job, one where they will not be withholding any of his wages. That's with Caster.

For his first pay, Ollie has taken a job recommended by one of the girls he once hooked up with Caster. She tells him she will have more work coming his way, as long as they continue to deliver. Since this is all Ollie does now, along with his deejay hustle, he can now spend some of his time reading and in the gym.

CHAPTER FOUR

Ollie and Caster continue working together, back and forth for a couple of years, but Caster never revealed his process to him. After Ollie met Deena at one of his private parties, he gradually stopped hanging out with Caster, dedicating more time to her until they finally lost contact.

Ollie has found a very smart and decent woman in Deena, a twenty-one-year-old art student, hoping to become a big artist one day. Unlike him, she comes from a broken family, so she finds it hard trusting men. She doesn't like Ollie's hustle with Caster, as she feels it's a sure way to end up dead or in jail.

To avoid losing her, he chooses her over his hustle. They date for a while before Ollie finally introduces her to his sister.

"Deena, what a lovely name.

"Where are you from Deena," Gloria asks as Ollie leaves them to catch up, while he grabs some dinner.

"We are from Zambani as well, Sunnyside, but we came here when I was two years old."

"Oh wow, Sunnyside, you guys must be loaded.

"No, not really."

"Ok, so who do you have in England then?"

"I have my father, stepmother and my younger sister, Nancy. I also have uncles and aunties here."

"Oh, ok. You come from a small family then?"

"Actually not, I also have step siblings, but I guess Nancy is the closest and most constant person in my life."

"You sound very English, do you speak any Chinga at all?"

"No, but I can understand some words, that's it."

"So, you are no good for my brother are you, Deena?"

"Well, he can teach me, if he wants me well enough."

"You are no use to us; our parents won't be able to communicate with you.

"What kind of Zambanian are you?"

"Aunty, play nice!"

"No, you are absolutely useless. "What was he thinking bringing you to me? "This is absolute nonsense. "I want you both out of my house when he comes back. "Rubbish people! "Couldn't he have found a nice white girlfriend if he wanted an English woman? "What a disgrace," she stops her runt hearing Ollie knocking on the door.

"Who is it?"

"It's me, your brother."

"Oh, hello brother, you're back already," as she opens the door and leans in for a kiss.

He goes straight to the kitchen where he puts the drinks in the freezer and places the pizza on the dining table. He goes back to the lounge only to find Deena with her arms folded and weeping. He looks at his sister who stands in the corner folding her arms and smiling, then looks at his girlfriend still weeping. She has broken her; this is the ugly shit called tradition.

New women joining the family get broken in, literally. Ollie bursts into laughter at first, filling the whole house with his hearty laugh. Deena looks at Ollie's face and realises she was stitched up; he knew this would happen.

After years of seeing his brothers' wives broken in, now it was his turn. He walks over to his girlfriend and picks her up from the sofa nestling her into his arms.

"I'm sorry mama, whatever she said, she didn't mean it. "It's just a horrible tradition that's all. "It's over now, it's over, let's go eat. "You have passed the worst phase, alright? "It will only get easier in time mama," he comforts her with the utmost respect, 'mama'.

"You need to apologise to Deena sis, she didn't deserve that," he said, harshly pointing his finger at Gloria. This protectiveness tells Gloria he loves her, she is special. Gloria on the other hand, has instilled fear and imposed her authority over her.

She has become the feared sister in-law who can derail her marriage plans. She is to be feared and spoiled with gifts, if she is to approve of Deena into the family. At the same time, it tells Deena she is safe and well protected by him. Gloria will soon pass her verdict, once the coast has cleared.

It is important for Ollie to know how Gloria feels about his wife to be. It's a simple but very complicated tradition they will pass on to their children for generations. The final verdict? Gloria likes Deena, a lot. She is smart and beautiful and feels he has found a decent wife in her.

Following Gloria's approval of Deena, Ollie and Deena are visiting her father to pitch his marriage proposal to him. Even though he and Deena have been seeing each other for a short while, Ollie feels he has no time to drag things longer than necessary.

The pressure from his father to get married is mounting on him. It is nerve wrecking on both Ollie and Deena who both know this is what they want. Linda has tagged along just for moral support. It is tradition that she learns how these things are done, for she soon could be following suit.

There is an uncle and an aunt who have come to witness this event.

"How are you baba? I am honoured to be in your presence," said Ollie, while on his knees, keeping his head down to avoid eye contact with his father-in-law as it's a sign of disrespect.
"Get off the floor, we don't do that here. Sit on the sofas please, you are embarrassing me."
"My apologies baba."
"Ah, embarrass you? This is our culture, brother! What has gotten into you?" said Deena's aunt, feeling ashamed of her brother.
"My house, my rules sister," he said calmly, while clicking away on his phone. I never understood all those village practices anyway, I was not raised like that. We are in England now, and as such, let's do as the English do," he said, looking at Ollie from above the frames of his thick glasses.

He looks down and continues swiping away on his phone. "We welcome you, Ollie. "Where are you from, if you don't mind me asking," said the aunt.
"I come from the Mandara West Province, N'ongwa. I am of the Kokwa tribe."
"Wow, N'ongwa. That's home to the most powerful spirits, do you know about them too," asked the uncle, keen to learn more.
"Yes, the Lion Spirit, hence the name, N'ongwa. "Thank you for your interest, uncle." They both smile as the uncle looks to his cousin who is not phased, one bit.
"So, are there no women of similar characteristics in your village, why are you dragging my daughter into all this stone age stuff," asked Deena's father who looks at Ollie awaiting his comeback line.
"Ollie checks with aunty to see if it's alright to engage with his father-in-law on this topic. Aunty nods, granting him permission to sell himself.

"Well, our tradition teaches us to look beyond our territory for marriage, that way we add diversity to our culture as a country," he said, checking with the uncle, who nods in agreement.

"Well, my daughter is not for sale, especially to someone I have not yet gotten to know," said the father, as he looks around the room to seal his last word.

"Brother, our children are old enough to choose who they wish to marry, soon it will be Linda bringing another son in law too. "What message are you sending to them? "Will you keep all your daughters to yourself? "This is despicable! "Give the young man a chance, otherwise why are we here on this day," she storms out, and so does Deena, her sister and stepmother trying to deescalate the situation.

"I am sorry you feel that way baba. "Uncle, I am sorry if I have offended you with my proposal. "I really love your daughter, and I wish for nothing else but your reconsideration. "I will await your response; may I be excused."

"Wait young man, before you leave just know this, I don't know you yet. "Neither do I know your people, and for that reason, I really need time to consider your proposal. "It's not like we are in Africa, where you'd bring me some kind of wealth.

"As you can see here, this is my very own castle. "I am very comfortable here, so it's not a question of wealth, it's a question of principle. "These are my principles; I will not be giving away my daughter to someone that I do not know. I have only met you a few times, but I still don't know you. "I hope you understand." He sits down and hand signals to Ollie, he has said enough. Uncle nods, excusing Ollie.

Ollie bows, then leaves the lounge to put his shoes on. He grabs his keys and leaves the house. Uncle follows and walks him to the car as he tries to calm him down and reassure him that he will put in a good word on his behalf. As he waits in the car, he sends a text message to Deena asking the two ladies to get ready to leave, but Deena and her sister are not ready to leave. They cannot leave like this. They tell him to come back for them later in the evening, as they need to catch up with their aunty and uncle.

It's been a few months since Ollie last saw or contacted Caster who has decided to get his man back. He has visited Ollie at his residence. He takes him on a road trip to Portsmouth harbour, where they walk around the crowded coast before driving to nearby Hayling Island, exploring the beautiful English seaside. By the time he finally drops Ollie off at home, he has managed to talk him into working with him again. He has promised to show him how he processes his money, only if he stays patient.

Ollie has no choice; he needs the money badly, as another employer has stopped him from working after they could not verify his national insurance either. With the big money coming from the bank jobs, Ollie is now saving for a luxurious wedding. He wants to get married to Deena within the next six months. He will not risk losing her, as he knows good gems like her are a rare find.

Deena is a good Christian girl, an academic and a beautiful woman all round. Unlike the tall women he is accustomed to in his mother, and sisters, she is way shorter, but he feels at home with her and wants to commit. Not only is she beautiful, but he also sees his mother's qualities in her. It is for all these reasons; he has decided she is a keeper. With his doubtful visa situation, he also believes getting married to a British citizen might come in handy one day, if things were to ever go south.

They both start laughing as it's a relief they both needed.

"Why did you do that," she asked, staring into his brown eyes.

"You needed relief and so did I, in the end."

"Yeah, but you refused to just fuck me, why?"

"Look, it's not my job to take away your virginity. "That's not fair on you and your sister both."

"Ah, I hate you. No one is better qualified to break this pussy than you. "Please, just fuck me. "I want it to be with you. "Why won't you just fuck me and get it out of the way, I don't want to be in my twenties and still be a virgin. It's like failure in life."

"Sorry, gotta go," he said, wrapping himself with a towel.

"Why are you still covering up, I have already seen everything."

"Well, we don't want your sister thinking anything ever happened between us now, do we?"

"Well, I won't tell if you don't," she shouts as he slums her door on his way out.

With all the fun and games Ollie is using as a distraction, the financial burden soon gets to Ollie and he decides he needs a new hustle quick. Caster has just the job, a smash and grab job. It has been a marvellous honeymoon period that is coming to an end.

Linda has gone back to her parents' house to spend Christmas with them. Marriage is starting to take its toll on Ollie and Deena. They simply cannot keep living in isolation anymore. The work, play and church routines are getting tiresome now. Deena wants more out of her life, but Ollie seems too comfortable in his little bubble.

She does not want to settle for a career as a healthcare assistant. Instead, she wants to go back to university to study adult nursing, since she has failed to get a job as an artist. She encourages Ollie to get himself enrolled into college and study whatever he likes, but he gets too defensive every time the subject arises.

CHAPTER FIVE

With more work coming his way, Dj Skee has passed a job down to Ollie. One of the teen parties he was meant to play has been double booked with a well-paying club job. Knowing what a great job he did with the former Nigerian president's birthday party; he no longer has doubts in his skillset. He will be passing all the cheap jobs to Ollie, so he can make a name for himself, from now on.

Deena is working nights. Whether she was working or not, she would still not go with Ollie. She hates witnessing the 'eye fucks' he gets from the ladies when he is playing. Still without transport of his own, Ollie has asked to borrow Caster's car as he is not available to help him due to a bad cold. He gives him the car but asks Ollie to take his sister along, in case the police stop him. Ollie is up for the babysitter job.

While at the party, Nancy sticks with him, sitting beside him all night, only leaving to fetch drinks, food and on toilet breaks. With Nancy sitting by his side all night, Ollie is safe from the ladies who figured he has one hell of a model girlfriend. To seal the party with a bang, Ollie plays a slow jam and asks the audience to grab a dance partner and leave it all on the dance floor.

He encourages Nancy to enjoy herself and dance with the young man that's been eyeballing her all night, but she is not moved. He takes her hand and dances with her instead. She floats and glides in his arms like the wind, while keeping eye contact with him at all times. Being that close to her, as he looked deeply into her soul, Ollie is left mesmerised by her beauty, but he manages to keep his composure.

As the party comes to a halt at midnight, Ollie, being the deejay, has a room already paid for by the hosts at a nearby Holiday Inn. He does not favour the hustle of being pulled over by the traffic police at stupid o'clock in the morning, as he has no licence, and he doesn't know the car owner's full details.

So, he curves in on the hotel room offer after consulting with Nancy. When they get to the hotel, he asks her to take the bed while he sleeps on the sofa in the corner. Nancy goes into the bathroom for a late-night shower. She will not sleep well without taking one. It helps her wind down, apparently.

Ollie is hardly trying to sleep. He is curious to see how she looks coming out of the shower. He waits and waits, until he starts to fall asleep. Suddenly, the shower stops. His heart switches on, and the blood starts to flow again.

His heart beats so loud under all the layers of chest muscle that he is afraid the young lady will hear it. The door handle clicks, and he squints his eyes, pretending he is asleep. He looks at the bottom of the bathroom door and awaits her foot to show first. She shuts the door before coming out. She gurgles some water and gently lets it out, while he expected a loud spit. Such a fucking lady!

His heart continues thudding away. Finally, the door handle clicks again, as she finally comes out. There it is, her divine foot, at last. He follows it up, past the ankle. She has such slender shins, long shins matter of fact. The white towel wrapped around her obstructs the rest. Fuck! Only the slender long arms, shoulders and neck are exposed, as her short, wet hair is tied in a towel. She finally snaps out of slow motion and walks up to him and gently taps his cheek with the palm of her hand.

"Oi, go take a shower.

"It's really nice."

"Me, why?"

"Yes, you.

"You smell of cigarettes from the party.

"I have left a towel and some soap in there for you.

"Be quick, I want to get some sleep." They continue to exchange whispers.

He goes into the shower where he quickly undresses, showers and wraps the towel around his waist before storming back into the room.

"You are wet," she chuckles, as she rubs some body cream on her back leaving her perky breasts deliberately exposed.

"You rushed so much that you forgot to dry yourself."

"Oh, sorry," he said as he sussed her mood. He continued walking towards the edge of the bed where she sits. Seeing the impression of his flaccid dick under the towel, she smiles and looks down as she pretends she did not see anything.

"It's ok, come, let me help you dry," as she starts to unwrap his towel.

"Are we ok like this," he asks, as he remembers she was a bridesmaid at his wedding, a short while back.

"Yes, we are ok like this," she reassures him, fully dismissing his worries.

"I am nervous," as he holds on to the towel that is halfway undone.

"I am excited," she responds, fully revealing his dick.

"I think he likes you," referring to his now charging dick.

"I think so too," as she grabs it, having a feel of its weight.

"He is heavy, such a big boy," as she kisses it on the tip ever so gently. She makes her first attempt at sucking him off. With her mouth warm and salivating, she triggers a shiver down his spine, reawakening all his senses.

"Oh," he groans, submitting to her.

"Is that ok, it's my first time," she asked before she continued sucking him off.

The whispering stops as she gets to work. He looks at her in utter disbelief this is happening to him. She is intimidatingly stunning. Slim, light skinned, long necked and wide eyed. Being slim, she is sharp around the edges but fluffy where it matters most. The head is good, but the power of his self-doubt and disbelief that it is truly her; this gorgeous young woman guiding his dick in and out of her mouth, that exacerbates the experience making him ejaculate too quickly. She did not expect it so soon.

The surprise cum-shot made her pull away, leaving him spewing all over her face and titties. She is shocked at the horror, but she stays calm as she continues jerking him off, letting it all spew out. She goes back into the shower and washes off his cum. He joins her in the shower and begins exploring her perfectly designed body while maintaining small talk.

"I am sorry, I came on you."

"It's fine, I was in the way.

"It was either me or the wall I guess."

"You are funny, I like that.

"So, when did you discover that you fancied me?"

"When I first saw you on my brother's social media."

"I cannot believe I was so blind all this time. You are so gorgeous, yet I never thought anything of you, because you were always his baby sister. How old are you though?"

"If you had known, would you still have married her?"

"Yes, I never saw you that way to be honest.

"Besides, your brothers would not have allowed it."

"Why, you think they don't want me to be happy?"

"Nah, we just have a lot of history between us, and I am like family to them."

"No, you are not. Certainly not to Goldie."

"What, he doesn't like me?"

"Let's just say, he sees through you."

"See what exactly?"

"He thinks you're one to watch, that's all."

"Me, why? when he is the ultimate gangster."

"He just thinks you're too smart, that's all."

"Really, that's volumes coming from him."

"I think he is right, maybe that's why you married Deena.

"I know you saw me all this time, you just played it safe."

"Safe how?"

"With a submissive wife."

"You think? Anyway, you still are not answering my question."

"I am nineteen, and you?"

"Fuck, I'm twenty-four."

"What, you didn't know I was old enough did you?

"You should have just asked."

"I certainly did not know that, and you should have said something. "Is that why you guarded me at the party, to keep the other ladies away?"

"I was enjoying myself sitting beside you, Mr Deejay, and it was supposed to be a kids party anyway."

"Teen party you mean, like people your age?"

"Whatever, we are here now, naked, and I am so turned on right now," she continues kissing him softly.

"There is Deena though, and I am way older than you."

"That's fine by me. "I'm not attracted to Deena, and neither am I attracted to boys my age anyway. "I am only attracted to you, my handsome man."

"Oh yeah," as he continues touching and caressing her body.

He turns her around, positioning himself behind her. He lowers himself, allowing his erect dick to get between her thighs. Its natural upward curve allows it to slide onto the lips of her warm pussy. Feeling him hot and hard, she wants him. She holds onto the wall, backing up into him.

He soaks up in her juices, slightly poking at her. She starts to moan as he gently tip-teases her when suddenly, he feels her hymen blocking his entrance.

"You are a virgin?"

"Yes."

"Wow, you don't say."

"I told you it was my first time, when I was giving you head."

"Shit, that's what you meant?"

"Yes."

"This is special, come to the bed."

He comes out of the shower and covers her in a towel. He wraps one around himself as he carries her back into the bedroom. He lays her on the bed and gently unwraps her towel which he folds and places under her buttocks. He kisses her ever so gently, making sure she still consents.

He progressively moves down to the perky breasts he so wanted to see. He moves down to her flat stomach caressing it and kissing her belly button. She oohs and aahs, as he caresses her inner thighs. She spreads her legs wider, welcoming him and encouraging him on.

He stares and adores her for a minute, then gently starts to tip-tease her with his tongue. The more she gets stimulated the more she lubricates. He is only happy to swallow her sweet juices. He swipes his tongue upwards and suckles her clitoris. He tips his tongue into her lips and suckles them too. He suckles her clit, clicking his tongue until she begs him to take her, she is ready and so is he.

Giving her head has left him all drippy. He crawls over her gorgeous body and looks into her eyes as his curved dick finds the source of her intoxicating pheromones. She nods, to tell him he can take it. He tip teases her, further relaxing her and building up the suspense before he finally digs into her, shuttering her hymen.

The head of his dick is tightly wrapped inside her as he starts wiggling and penetrating deeper into her tight pussy. The bleeding and stinging quickly stops as she naturally lubricates through each stroke, making the full accommodation easier.

She holds on to him, at times digging her nails deeper into his skin, scratching his back. Bad kitty! She moans and kisses him as she draws him in deeper then pushes him out as her pain overpowers her pleasure.

"You're too big, it hurts so much," she pleads with him.

"Should I stop," he asks.

"No. "It is nice. It's really amazing. "I can't tell which is more, the pain or the pleasure. "Keep going. "More, faster. "Slow down, you are hurting me. "Harder, faster. "You're too much. "Gently please. "Faster, deeper, harder. "I gotta pee, I gotta pee. "Stop, I need to pee!"

He lets her empty her bladder, then tells her to just let it go next time, as it's not pee but a squirt that she feels building up - a more potent type of orgasm. He lays on his back, towel under his buttocks and lets her control the ride. She rides him fast and slow, deep and shallow as he grabs her ass, guiding her in stimulating her g-spot with his head.

She starts exploding on him, one after the other, until she finally collapses on him. He flips her over and gives her a deep thrusting. "Gently please," she pleads with him. "Faster, deeper, harder," she continues guiding him along as she savours the moment she had long imagined with him. It is on her terms. This is her day. She has become a woman today. Finally, he timely unloads inside her as they cum at the same time.

She whimpers as her last gash has caused her freshly perforated hymen to sting. She giggles hysterically, as the oxytocin buzzes through her brain. She has forgotten all about the pain of losing her virginity, like a mother welcoming her baby after giving birth. She has lost her virginity to a good man. She has had her first multiple orgasms experience. For now, sex is good.

He watches her as she lays there peacefully asleep, Ollie knows he has crossed the line. His friendship with Caster might be coming to an end. They know each other too well to be in the same room after this.

Ollie had become used to the old system over the years. They hand him the job application forms and he fills them in, submits them and awaits their calls for work. This time however, the great recession is in progress, employees are being made redundant left right and centre. The world's economy is so bad, but here at home, it's so bad for the British citizens that politicians are using the hot topic of immigration to get the people's support.

Any news channel you watch you hear, "immigrants are taking our jobs," "immigrants are taking our housing," "immigrants are taking our benefits". This hate rhetoric is really making Britain a nasty place to be for most foreigners but not for Ollie, he looks and sounds English.
He had mastered how to take advantage of his good looks, charm and mesmerising smile. In all his previous

employment, he had always brought the pipe to the table. He had figured ladies out based on how they always paid him attention, complementing his physic and eyeballing his bulge.

He was a very likable guy; people always had a blast working with him. In his current job, he worked his way up, from dining area attendant to shift manager in a big restaurant chain. As always, you could never beat Ollie to discovering an opportunity whenever one arose. The temptation of seeing money everywhere had once again gotten the best of him. As the saying goes, 'what goes around comes around'.

Ollie is called up to the meeting room upstairs. The regional manager is chairing the meeting. The restaurant manager and his other shift managers are also present. There is another junior member of staff in there.

As soon as he walks in, he senses the tension, as it whips his memory back to the amusement park with Sarah. He has been here before; he stays calm, smiles and respectfully greets everyone in the meeting room. No one smiles back at him, sending a clear message to him, this is not fun and games. Swords have been drawn.

The regional manager cuts to the chase and plays two CCTV clips showing exhibit A, Ollie taking money from the till and walking off to the back of the kitchen. Exhibit B, the other kid also taking money from the till and walking to the back.

He unrolls the printed long till records, which shows exhibit C, Ollie's till totals before and after the voided transactions and same for the other kid on exhibit D. He tells Ollie and the kid, this is strong evidence that they have both been stealing money and that they are immediately suspended until a decision has been made.

For now, the meeting wraps up with the two suspects handing in their uniforms and name badges. The case will be presented to the head office where a decision will be made whether police should be contacted, or they are simply released from their contracts.

CHAPTER SIX

Ollie knows too well when it is time to move on. He goes on a job hunt, just like routine. The only thing different this time is, the government has come up with a political agenda and a set of new laws helping to crack down on illegal workers and tax evaders. Passports, work permits, or national insurance were never discussed at any of his previous job interviews, until now.

No employer can hire without vetting the applicant's papers. They have been supplied with tech such as UV light scanners for holograms and watermarks, and hotlines for checking the validity of passports, work permits and student visas. With the limited jobs available only prioritised for British citizens, the checks are very stringent.

Ollie had an indefinite leave to remain that his cousin had acquired for him back in St Albans. He had brought his passport, bank card, and a national insurance card, all ready to hand. The interview had gone well, and he had been hired as a night shift supervisor for a local supermarket.

The paperwork check and recording of documents was going well, until the recruiting manager shouted some very rude words. He walked back towards Ollie and threw his passport on his lap instructing him to get out of his office. Ollie tried reasoning with him, to understand what the problem was, but the insulting man offered no explanation.

He mattered mostly rude words, "forged visa" and "illegal immigrants". This was the day real nightmares besieged him, but what does one lose when he has lost everything? He has finally found out that the visa in his passport is a fake.

This is criminal. Who could ever do such a heinous act? His cousin had paid a lot of money to this immigration lawyer. Did he just print off visas without recording them in the system or was he just a poser selling forged documents?

There are a lot of questions to ask but who does he ask? He goes over many scenarios in his head, as he takes the long walk from Guildford to Godalming where he resides with Deena. It has not even been a year; how does he tell his newly wedded wife such bad news?

He calls his sister Gloria and breaks the news to her first. She is shell shocked and goes into a panic binge drink. He does not drink so this is a very numbing experience. His best friend Caster has no words either, not even I told you so. This is a very dark time indeed, but Ollie takes his mother's old wisdom and accepts it as an opportunity to learn and for growth.

He gets home and soaks in the bath creating a million entry points to the conversation with Deena. He plays some music and prepares dinner while waiting for her to finish her twelve-hour shift at their local care home. His fingers start to tremble, as he hears her locking up her bicycle in the tool shed just behind the kitchen.

Carers never have a good twelve-hour shift, there is no better angle to approach her from, but run her a hot foamy bath and present her with the hearty meal he has prepared. She appreciates the hard work but asks him to join her in the bathtub.

He joins in, sits and listens to her ranting. He remains quiet, occasionally taking deep breaths, as he assesses her mood. He finally summons the courage and breaks the news to her and patiently waits for her response. She abruptly gets up, wraps up with a drying towel and skips dinner for bed.

She tosses and turns and takes deep breaths every few minutes until she turns to him to get a few things off her chest.

"Did you know the visa was fake all these years?"

"No, why?"

"Why? I could go to jail for this.

"I could be treated as an accomplice to this.

"This is fraudulent!"

"What, what is fraudulent?

"What are you on about?"

"Us, our marriage!

"It looks like you married me for my papers, when you knew."

"Wait, stop accusing me here. "I am just as shell shocked as you are."

"Nah, excuse my language, but that's bullshit, and you know it!

"To be honest, I have always suspected something was off about you."

"Off, how?"

"I mean, why would someone as smart as you are, with an indefinite visa, not enrol into a college and get an education? "I mean, everyone in our age group is chasing a career right now, but no, not you. "It doesn't make no fucking sense. "Just saying!"

"When did you start feeling like that?"

"I have had my moments, like right now. "Why are you not even freaking out at this situation we are in? "You're just too calm for my liking. "Which is making me nervous as fuck!"

"What moments? "Are you here to have moments or be a good submissive-wife? "Do you honestly think I only married you for your papers? "I actually believed I had my own, thank you!"

"Babe, I'm just saying, it looks suspicious from my viewpoint. "Calm the fuck down and stop poking at me, Jesus!"

"Now you are just asking for trouble. "What viewpoint is that? "And do not fucking tell me to fucking calm down after you have dumped all this inflammatory shit on me! "Come here! "Get your little ass up!"

Hearing the anger in his voice, she makes a dash for it. "Aw, you are hurting me!" she pleads as he grabs her by the neck.

"Please stop!

"Stop hurting me!

"Please, I am sorry!"

"Who do you think you're talking to, using filthy language like that? "I am your husband, not your fucking little brother, you hear me! "Who has been feeding you all this shit? "Coming in here with that challenging behaviour! "Why don't you feel sorry for me? "Who the fuck are you, right now? "You're supposed to be on my side!"

What he does not realise at this point, is his loss of self-control. His temper and rage have taken charge. As he is screaming at her, it's no longer a verbal dialogue, but has escalated into physical violence. He is now talking with his fists; all these questions are only in his head. She hangs on to dear life, as she keeps uttering, "sorry, sorry".

Sorry is the only word that requires a lesser effort, in her now diminished state. He has reached a moment of pure adrenaline, where inflicting pain has become an art. He is so absorbed in the smell of her blood and the thud of his fists striking her fragile little frame.

She collapses to the floor, where she continues to absorb the impact of his blows. Feeling every strike and every blow of his own fists, he feels he is at the epitome of superior dominance over her. Her begging for forgiveness resonates with a desperate last howl of a prayer in death.

He finally notices the blood covering his fists then snaps out of hysteria and looks at Deena's body, curled into a ball by the front door. She had just made it to the locked front door, but she could not escape. She is conscious but beat. She feared this day may come, but the good times outweighed the inevitable danger that lurked in the shadows.

He stops feeling sorry for himself and carries her to the bathroom where he lays her into the cold bath to prevent swelling. She keeps apologising to him as though it's her fault she got a beating. She emphasises that, had she only let a lying dog sleep; none of this should have happened. He apologises to her too for losing his temper and offers to make her a hot chocolate to keep her warm in the cold bath.

She has suddenly gone from being a boxing opponent to a pampered queen of his heart. He wraps her in a drying towel and carries her to the bed, where he brings her reheated dinner and a cup of Rooibos tea. She can't seem to chew as her jaws hurt and her tongue is cut.

The spicy food makes the open cuts bite. He apologises and reassures her that he was the victim in all of this. He had never knowingly used her, misled her or anyone fully knowing his visa was a fake. After an exhausting and painful evening, she finally asks him to cuddle her. They spoon up and slip into dreamland.

The week off work has helped stable the ship. Deena is a bit more energised this morning and her bruises have fully cleared. She has made a big halal breakfast topped with freshly made crepe, waffles and squeezed grapefruit juice.

As soon as he sits up for breakfast in bed, she leaps into advisor mode. Apparently, her sister who is in the process of seeking asylum, has suggested they either apply for a spouse's visa since she is British, or he applies for asylum too, before they stop granting refugee status to Zambanians.

The idea is a great one, most Zambanians in their church got refugee status so the advice is readily available, if ever needed. He agrees to prioritise this refugee route, but he looks mortified, for he never wanted to drag this innocent soul into his reckless ways.

However, she gives him tremendous support and plans to fast and pray over the tough journey ahead. For now, she continues to take up extra night shifts at work, to balance things around the home. Unable to work or socialise, Ollie feels caged as he is having to go all out, to show her he is trying.

It doesn't take too long before Ollie goes back to working with Caster, so that he can contribute something to the table, as he feels dick alone cannot get them through these hard times. He is entrusted with depositing cheques at the banks and collecting Caster's cut once the money has cleared.

It's big money for the both of them. Caster is smart enough for a street thug, but Ollie just needs work experience in order to thrive in this field. They keep Caster's business going while he is finding out more information for his asylum application.

He quickly learns the most important part of Caster's hustle. He gets corrupt postmen into his pockets, paying them upwards of two hundred quid a pop. The postmen know which envelopes contain tax refund cheques, identity documents and benefits information. With the right team of postmen working for him, Ollie starts running his own hustle.

He gets envelopes dropped off at one of his addresses, prints off cheques with the cheque number intended for someone else and alters the sum. He deposits them into a preferred bank account, waits for the money to clear then withdraws all the money splitting it in the middle with the consenting account holder.

Ollie sees a lot of potential in the identity information which sells like hot cakes. Illegals mainly buy birth certificates and British driving licences to apply for British passports. His loyal crew do all the hard work. He never handles anything personally, and he advises his crew to always wear gloves while working. He knows it is only a matter of time before the new biometric system soon catches up.

With the new money coming in, Ollie has bought a subtle MK1 Suzuki Jimny, for dropping off and picking up his wife from work this winter. Caster gives him his details to register it in, in case he ever gets pulled over by the traffic cops. These new ANPR police cameras are getting a lot of bad people off the roads, with illegals being deported.

Last week, one of Ollie's boys got picked up driving his brand-new Mercedes S Class without a licence and is now facing deportation. He had tax, insurance and MOT but the arresting officer thought he looked way too young for the car. When they ran his details, he had no licence registered with the DVLA.

Ollie had told these young boys to be subtle, but what do they do? Buy BMWs, Benzes and Bentleys without evidence of a legitimate income. The police officers can't even afford these shiny toys, that's why they gladly take them away as proceeds of crime.

CHAPTER SEVEN

Today, Ollie is at Lunar House Croydon, submitting his asylum application. He has brought his passport and birth certificate as proof of identity and to show good faith as most of these asylum seekers don't even use their real details. The lady who bags up his documents just writes his name on the envelope and calls the next one. People are being processed like mail here. No empathy or time for touchy feely. He spends the whole day waiting to be called in, but nothing happens.

He has been here since eight o'clock this morning and now it's quarter to four. There are only two other people left to be processed, when one of the officers comes to get him. He sits in the chair on the other side of the wooden desk with a glass between them. The officer takes out an orange form from his cabinet drawer and asks a very few but specific questions. Date of birth, date of arrival in the UK, point of entry, reason for coming here and why he is seeking asylum.

The room is not cold but when nerves kick in, he starts trembling in his voice. He is offered some water, but he declines. He just wants to escape now; this whole thing just feels off. His gut feeling is screaming run, this is all a mistake, but he hangs in there. He knows given the heavy security in here, he will only get out when they let him. The officer has all the answers he needs from him, so he gives him an orange appointment letter to come back for an interview in three weeks.

It is the longest train ride back to Godalming, but he understands sometimes power changes hands. As of this moment, they have the power over him. He gets home and recharges his Blackberry as soon as he walks into the house. He starts going over all the BBMs from Deena. He calls her and updates her on the day. She was worried sick that something terrible might have happened over there.

Tonight, is ovulation night and as such intimacy is a must! When she finally gets home, Deena sets the mood with some candles and some Musiq Soulchild. The candles burn away, filling the room with their strawberry scent.

They kiss passionately while undoing each other's robes. She throws him over the bed and pounces on him. She assumes the cowgirl position and takes her time interlocking fingers while caressing him so ardently. She looks him in the eyes as she seeks his approval to go down on him.

With his nod, she caresses him on her way down. She blows soft kisses on the tip of his drenching and fully engorged dick. She sucks him off gently as he groans and curls up his toes.

She knows he is in a world of immense pleasure by the mouthfuls of pre-ejaculate she is swallowing. This is all about her tonight, she raises her head and slowly climbs over him. He is so engorged that she needs not to help him find the warm and leaky opening tucked away between her thighs.

She positions her dripping pussy over the tip of this most coveted banana dick and starts accommodating him. The intensity of both pleasure and pain makes it all the worthwhile. She keeps to a steady and slow rhythm until she feels fully stretched out. She pauses for a minute, absorbing the stretching sensation radiating through her chest cavity.

She starts grinding on him, tucking it deeper into the back if her stretched out pussy. He is holding on by the thread as the pleasure intensifies. He wants to get the first one out of the way, but she is also building up for a big and splashy squirt as she moans so loudly that it feels the whole house.

He positions the towel beneath his buttocks and prepares for a warm-silky gash. As she focuses the tip of his dick on to her g-spot, her pussy walls tighten up and get even more rigid making it impossible for him to hold on. He manages to just hang in there until she gets her first explosion out of the way.

She has soaked him up good, but now needs to regroup. She slumps onto his chest. He squeezes her sweet-plump buttocks and suckles on her hardened nipples while she rests on his pulsating dick.

It is a much-needed break for him but the licking and suckling of nipples is making her want more of him. With their eyes locked onto each other, she slowly twerks on his tip making him even harder.

She gently strokes his full length combining with a back-and-forth grind. He feels her tightly wrapped around his full length. She takes him way deeper into the 'back room' as she watches his facial expressions. Deep penetration like this won't hurt her as long as it is kept gentle and smooth.

He just needs a few hard strokes, and he will burst. She does not let him off that easily. This is where she teaches him all about discipline, stamina and savouring the pussy. She takes his palm and places it way above her belly button whispering to him, "you are right here, this is where I feel your dick". She rides him in different strokes and pace while controlling his eagerness to release. When she feels his dick pulsating, she slows down, and when he stands firm, she rides him like a runaway slave, squirting on him.

The catching towel is soaked through, she is deeply satisfied. She rides him deep and fast and lets him explode inside her. She slumps to his chest once more, catching her breath as his dick kicks through the ejaculation process like a dying horse. It is in these ovulation moments of shared oxytocin release that Ollie and Deena, like many other fighting couples, make the strongest of bonding.

The day of the appointment is upon him, Ollie is on the train to Croydon again. He has his BlackBerry, wallet and train ticket. Back at home, Deena is asleep as she has come from a night shift and is going back again tonight. Ollie checks through security and awaits his interview. No one attends to him until around half past three when three street looking immigration officers come to get him.

They take him to a far corner and ask him to confirm his details. They read him his rights and place him under arrest for possession of forged identity documents. He is taken to the local police station where he is kept overnight awaiting trial the next day at Croydon's magistrate court.

He is numb, he had anticipated for the worst, worst is here now. He is feeling cold from a combination of the cold holding cells and nerves. He does not get a phone call to Deena, as the police are busy processing other customers.

The next morning, he is given his belongings and taken to the magistrate's court. He is held up in the cold basement cells where he gets a visit from a government lawyer, who informs that he may not get seen today as the courts are so busy.

She also advises him that he is being charged with, "possession of a falsely acquired identity document with intent to deceive". If he is found guilty, he may be looking at ten years imprisonment under the Identity Card Act.

The level of calmness he feels can only be reached by a Yoga Sensei. No amount of scaremongering is going to fuck up his calmness now. At the end of the day, he is escorted into the courtroom where the panel tells him the magistrate court is not competent with his level of crime.

His crime falls under the terrorism act, something that only the crown court are able to pass judgement on. However, due to the intricacies of his situation and the nature of his crime, they fear he may reoffend again if they let him back into the community.

Based on those facts, they recommend police custody until he gets a court date arranged. He no longer qualifies for the local police station, so he sits on the small bus with tinted windows, en route to HMP High Down.

He is processed, assigned a prisoner number and a shared cell at High Down. He is in with two African men in their mid-forties who help him get his phone call with Deena. She is left distraught at the confirmation of her worst nightmare.

He apologises that he never intended for this to happen, and that he never wanted her dragged into this mess. He gives her his new address and contact procedures. They cry together but the call is short.

His cell mates seem calm. One is still in here indefinitely even though he finished serving his six-year sentence. They will keep him until he is proven safe for release back into the community. He was caught at Gatwick with just over two kilos of snow, while returning from Colombia. The other man is starting his twenty-three-year sentence for a double manslaughter.

When they ask Ollie what he is in for, he has to really impress, so he tells them he is in for armed robbery which he is very knowledgeable about. Here, you need to earn respect and fast. There are just way too many youths carrying shanks in here, looking to prove their gangster and make a name for themselves.

Now at his fully grown size of 6'4," Ollie is not really a small guy. He is not worried about the youths as he can and loves a good scrap. It's not long before the youths start referring to him as 'Big Man'. When they see him in the lounge, they bring him gifts of the gold dust that is salt and pepper.

In return, all they ask for is protection in the showers, and in the exercise area where they are most vulnerable. The food here is tasteless, so the salt and pepper really are a good deal.

There are no chefs here, all labour is covered by the prisoners themselves. The prison stewards are prisoners who offer information to first timers like him. He speaks to one, who is serving indefinitely. His fifteen-year sentence finished two years ago, but he is being held until proven safe for return to the community.

He tells him that he killed his mother's abusive boyfriend, then his mother too after she called the police on him. He seems very calm; besides, he was only seventeen when he committed the crime. He gives Ollie a tour of the place and gets him registered for the gym.

There are two envelopes on his top bunker, the slim brown envelope contains the much-anticipated court date which is in two weeks. The fat white one is a love letter from Deena. She has missed her regular doses of oxytocin and dopamine. She is now working out in preparation for his return. Also enclosed inside is a stamped return envelope.

His new cell mate asks for any details worthy of sharing. He is a very slim and soft-spoken east African man who got arrested at Heathrow Airport where he worked illegally as an airport security officer. He was employed by a very reputable security company.

His predicament was made worse by a deportation order, which is the reason why he is awaiting removal while he is in with murderers and armed robbers. Most of the days, he is just fasting and in energy preserving mode. He only gets loud with the tongues during his dawn prayers which takes forever.

Ollie is waiting to be escorted onto the bus. Court date is today. He is well excited, not for the outcome, but for the judgement day has arrived. Finally, he will know his fate by the end of the day.

There is a culture of self-representation here, which has been passed on to him. He has written a heartfelt letter to the judge, explaining the circumstances leading up to his arrest, pleading with the judge that he is only the victim of organised crime and not the perpetrator. When he is called in, the panel takes time to examine his letter, since it is all the evidence he has.

They are back just after ten minutes and have reached their decision. It comes as no surprise to Ollie, that the Home Office had filed for his Deportation Order, along with the heaviest crime they could pin on him. The judge tells him that he acknowledges his letter of plea and has taken into consideration the fact that up until this arrest, he had never been involved in any crime. This showed good outstanding character on his part.

However, the criminal charges against him are too severe and cannot go unpunished, under UK law. As a result, the judge recommends six months imprisonment, minus time already served prior to the court hearing. As for the deportation order, the judge feels the order is in breach of his human rights and as such, the deportation order is thrown out.

The fact that he had sought asylum before his arrest was all it took to make the deportation order illegal. They cannot deport a person at risk of persecution in his or her own country without examining their evidence. The session is concluded, and Ollie is taken back to High Down where he will serve the remainder of his sentence.

His new residence at High Down is a Category B prison, the second highest security prison below Cat A prisons like Belmarsh. Ollie knows this is serious jail time but remains optimistic for the opportunity this may bring. With Deena visiting today, it's a four-hour train ride from home, so Caster tags along and drives her there.

They arrive and are given visitors' vests and instructions, restricting physical contact with the prisoner, so his visitors sit across the bench with their hands on the table where they can be seen. She is just happy to see him. Conversation is kept clean due to Caster's presence. They say a quick prayer before the visiting time is up.

It is an emotionally draining experience that leaves her heart broken. His friend looks a bit saddened too, seeing his buddy in prison. He blames his wife for the ill advice to submit his identity documents to the Home Office.

Had he not submitted that passport with a forged visa in it, this would not have happened to him. He is only being criminalised because he showed good faith. He only wanted to prove his innocence, that he had not intentionally sought for the false visa and to prove his identity.

The Home Office on the other hand, are working hard to meet the figures set out by the government, to remove two hundred thousand illegals from their shores per year. He stayed at High Down for six weeks, during which the government provided him with a case worker and started working on his refugee application.

He also took this time to take GCSEs English and Maths, which he passed very well. At the end of his sixth week, he is called into the Governor's office. His early release application has been approved. He can now go home to Deena and finish his sentence of another six weeks on curfew. This is such sweet music to his wife's ears.

While Ollie was inside, Deena had been applying for a place to study adult nursing. She is over the moon after being offered a place at KCL. Commuting from Godalming to London Waterloo is not a choice, this calls for relocation, somewhere new.

She finds a few studio flats available to rent in Forest Hill and Sydenham, South East London. Ollie knows London very well, so she elects to work while he is entrusted with picking their suitable home for the next 3 years of her studies. He asks for a lift and gets picked up by Caster who takes him all over London, except where he needs to be.

Caster is thrilled his right-hand man is moving back to London. He is hopeful that, if Ollie's move to London is successful, business is back in full swing. Ollie is a major contributor to his business. He has connections to the church. His church colleagues have been the major account donors for Caster's business. Most of them have no papers, so the temptation of forty grand split two ways is inescapable.

OLLIE SAVAGE

What Caster doesn't know is, Ollie has his own plans besides playing middleman. He plans on re-establishing his own crew and creating his empire in the same kingdom. This type of business is not as territorial as the drug game, so both Ollie and Caster can flourish without ever bumping heads.

As the day goes by, Caster senses Ollie is somehow reserved. He is not himself. He needs to loosen up. Caster throws him a few feelers to see what's bothering him but gets nothing back, Ollie won't fully engage. Caster does not let that fuckup his Chi, he tells Ollie about how he has developed a taste for roulette. It's only befitting that he introduces Ollie to this high-stake game but warns him of the addiction that comes with it. They go into a casino where Caster buys some chips for the play.

To Ollie's surprise, Caster seems to have a natural talent for this game. He wins ten thousand pounds, sterling, in less than half an hour from his initial five hundred quid stake. Ollie is thinking about what he can do with his split once they have cashed out. He has his own go at other games, but he is not successful on any of them. He goes over to check on Caster who is in his moment, the winnings go up and down for far too long that Ollie loses interest.

Caster will not cash out his winnings. He starts talking about how much money he needs to get, in order to pay off his car and other financial commitments. Ollie feels he is planning ahead, it's an excuse to not share his winnings. In the end, he loses all his winnings, and another five grand of his own money. It's really bad, Ollie feels bad for him and lends him the two grand rent money Deena had given him. At least, if he wins back some of his money, he can pay back Ollie's two grand, surely.

64

They start off well. They go up to fifteen thousand but now Caster is feeling the rush again and starts talking about setting a twenty thousand record. He explains to Ollie that it's not really twenty grand he is winning, if he takes away the seven point five, they are already down today.

Besides, he claims that yesterday alone, he lost another ten grand. So, this is an opportunity to get it all back. Ollie is getting frustrated about the many excuses that keep coming up. Now he just wants to cash out and stick to what they are good at, at least they don't lose money at their own hustle.

Caster zones Ollie out, he has been at it for too long that the concentration is no longer there. He ends up losing all the money, again. To the last penny, again! Caster tells Ollie that he has never lost twice in a row on roulette, Ollie does not buy into the bullshit.

He is more concerned about how to explain losing this rent money to Deena. He is not even supposed to be hanging around the likes of Caster anymore. He brings unnecessary risk with everything that is going on with his asylum application. If Ollie winds up in trouble with the law again, it will ruin any chances he has at getting his refugee status.

He is also worried she may see this as sabotage, she is doing all she can to build a good life for them, while he is doing everything to derail that plan. He switches off his BlackBerry and sticks it out with Caster for the night. It has not been a bad day after all, if you forget the misfortune of losing a few grand.

This is the most fun Ollie has had since leaving prison and coming off his curfew last week. These two are ravaged, they go into Five Guys and sit down for a friendly competition. Five cheeseburgers and a large coke each, loser pays the bill. To save the loser humiliation, let's just say, Ollie ended up paying the bill.

They go to Caster's new flat in Marble Arch for the night, where Ollie sleeps on the sofa and tries his hardest to block out the shagging noises coming from upstairs. Early in the morning, he sneaks out and goes to the bank to get some money.

He gets on the tube and goes to view the studio flats as planned, but most are now gone except the one Deena was hopeful for on Taymount Grange, in the leafy suburbs of Forest Hill. He secures a deposit on it and sends a few BBMs to Deena who is ecstatic.

The flat is only five minutes away from Forest Hill train station and Sainsbury's, forty minutes away from King's College University and the hospital where she will be doing her placements.

There is also an added benefit of about an hour's walk to his sister's house in Camberwell. This really is going to be a fantastic new beginning for the both of them. So, for now, everyone else's problems can wait.

Ollie has been following the rules by not applying for work or seeking handouts. The asylum seekers rules clearly state, "no recourse to public funds". He settles for his husbandry duties in which he cooks, he eats, and he cleans. He washes, he irons, and he makes dinner.

Deena comes back in the evening, jumps in the bath and reads one of her many novels. After dinner they pray, consummate and go to bed. Routine, routine and more routine while Ollie's asylum application has not moved position one bit.

OLLIE SAVAGE

A year has passed, and his case has not been passed on to a case worker yet. Every week on a Tuesday, he goes to Electric House, Croydon for reporting - a track and trace system for the Home Office. It is very worrying reporting here. He has seen people come in to report and they get handcuffed and transported to a secret location for deportation.

Reporting at any of these immigration centres does not always equate to getting settlement, sometimes it means you are awaiting a seat to become available on your flight home. Many seekers bring a packed suitcase every time they report. The ones that do not, risk going home with just the clothes on their backs.

As he looks around him, he observes that these people do not hate their countries of origin. These people all have loved ones, families, friends even children back home. It's the fact that they came here with hope, that they can support their whole tribes back home once they get settled.

Based on their own accounts, some were at greater risk of being persecuted by their governments so they sold their land, businesses or properties and got out while they could. It's always shocking, watching police shooting civilians dead in the streets of some of these impoverished countries, but who sees the secret ambush killings or the genocides of a whole tribe of people?

CHAPTER EIGHT

Ollie has an impromptu meeting with Caster today. He agrees to meet up with him at his local betting shop. They gamble the afternoon away. Caster is taking things easy here due to the maximum spins rule. He can only spin a maximum of one hundred quid.

He wins just over ten grand and Ollie tussles with him and prints off the voucher. They cash the money in, but Caster keeps all the winnings for himself. He imposes an order on Ollie, either they go to the casino or he gets nothing from this morning's winnings.

Somehow, Ollie wants in on the casino fun, again. Home is becoming too boring, stuck with the misses and the daily routine. Besides, where better to spend his hard-earned money without questioning or raising suspicions. He is diligently test-driving Caster's brand-new Mercedes CLS500. It's not the grand theft auto style of driving this car is accustomed too. He cannot afford to draw any unnecessary attention to himself.

He loves the car, which comes standard with leather interior, a DVD player, auxiliary port, a low roaring set of AMG twin pipes and the massive 22s it sits on. The thing is a beast and pulls like one. It's not for Ollie, he is into the zero-tax type of vehicles, for the environment.

While swiftly cruising along the motorway, Caster opens up to Ollie about an opportunity he has coming up. He is putting together a team for a high stake, lower risk, smash and grab job. He reassures him that it's a safe job, nice and quick.

He has discovered the value of the new Audemars Piguet watches in this one joint. He needs help putting the project together and see how much they can make of it. Ollie knows too well these watches carry a life sentence. Just googling the brand name or searching for it on eBay makes you a police target.

Caster knows how to work around Ollie, he massages his ego and promises him gold. He even throws in his sister Nancy, in the mix, hoping to lure him in. The sister he baits him with, catches none of his attention. Nancy had a massive crush on Ollie but her older brother, Goldie, stood in the way as she was still coming of age.

It wasn't obvious to Ollie that Nancy was seventeen when he took her innocence. It was on the morning he took her home, that he discovered she had lied about her age. He had to find out the hard way, after he took a thorough beating from her older brother, Goldie. Given the brutal ass kick and her dishonesty, Ollie had to cut her loose.

Smash and grabs are an old classic and a niche that is under-utilised. You find your target, steal some getaway bikes, put on your kits and go in smashing security glass with harmers and bag some shit. They had done a few of these jobs with betting shops before, so Ollie knew what he was getting himself into.

Ollie is getting bossy, he does not like working under anyone. He likes being in control which is why when he accepts to work with Caster on this job, he sets the rules as he understands the risk involved. Caster agrees to let Ollie pick his own team and set his own parameters in place. To top it all, they both must play the central components in the job, that way, no one gets any ideas.

Ollie is home alone and bored in the house, when he decides to visit Pornhub, from his fifty-five-inch wall mounted smart tv. On the homepage is a slave themed video. The title alone draws Ollie to watch it.

The white girl in the video rides the black man like a true runaway slave. He immediately wants in on the action that he finds himself reaching for some wet wipes and a tub of coconut cream on his wife's dresser. He is interrupted by his ringing phone. There is an unsaved mobile number blinking on the screen. He answers nervously.

"Hi, Ollie here."

"What? "You didn't save my number, Ollie."

"Sorry, my lady, it must have slipped my mind.

"Seriously though, who is this?"

"I cannot believe you, bye Ollie!"

The young lady on the phone has her brother's temperament. It's Nancy, but Ollie is already preoccupied with the Pornhub scene. She waits a minute before she realises he has not called her back, for a whole minute. His phone rings again.

"Ollie, you may speak!"

"Oh, so now you know who I am.

"Why didn't you call me back?

"You're such a hater!"

"Come on baby, forgive a brother.

"Last time your crazy brother put a knee on my neck, for returning you home.

"Let's just say, I wasn't ready to die."

"I wasn't talking about that.

"I meant, why did you not call me back just now?"

"I wasn't sure you were alone."

"Don't worry, he is not here. "Besides, I'm a grown ass woman now. "Please forgive me for I lied to you, I was seventeen, but still legal."

"No worries, I have healed now.

"Besides, you have that to die for pussy."

"You sure know how to compliment a lady; I give you that."

"You know me, I'm a hustler baby. "But, I have missed you though. "How have you been?"

"Come on, you haven't missed me Ollie.

"You're stuck in there with that mafia wife of yours.

"She must be gangster to keep you down."

"Gangster, nah, not like you boo.

"You are the truth, next level badness."

"Really, you think I am bad?"

"Yeah, you're the truth boo.

"You know I have always said that Nancy."

"Yeah, when you took my virginity, you paedo."

"I remember you consenting."

"Of course.

"I was seventeen and stupid, fucking a married man.

"Maybe I should open a case against you, say you raped me."

"Too bad, this call is being recorded."

"Really," she hangs up and Ollie rings her back.

"You better not be fucking recording me this time, Ollie!"

"Nah, mama.

"Why would I do that to my sweet boo.

"I cannot do you like that, ever."

"You stupid man, that almost cost you another knee."

"I'm sorry mama, I wouldn't want that again, surely."

"Where is your wife, is she there?"

"Nah, she is always at work these days.

"You can come over.

"I've got something for you."

"What is it?"

"I won't tell you.

"I have to show you."

"Spare me, please.

"If I come all the way and waste my fuel for no reason, I will stab your black ass!"

"You are really crazy.

"You sound serious too."

"Nah, just playing.

"I won't cut you baby; mama won't cut her baby."

"Oh, so I am baby now, huh?"

"Who is your mama, huh?"

"You mama, I love you too mama."

"Get out of here with that bullshit!

"If you loved me, you'd tell me what you've got for me up in them burbs you now live in."

"Wait until you see it.

"Just come and get it for yourself."

"Yeah, what's your postcode then?"

"I have texted it to you.

"Flat fourteen."

"Ok then gangster, better not get me all excited for nothing."

"Never! "Let me shower quickly and tidy up."

"Why, is your ass trying to fuck me on the first day back?

"Good thing I'm on my period.

"Let's keep talking then because it isn't happening."

"Really, is your period psychic? "Shit"

"I knew it, I knew it, knew it, knew it.

"A man only has got you something when his dick is rocket hard.

"Open the door then, let me in then."

"What, no way," as he opens the door.

"Hey mama," said Ollie, as the two kiss and tightly embrace in each other's arms.

It's a long embrace before giving each other a stare down, expressing their longing for one another.

"Hey Mama, how come you got here so quickly?" asked Ollie as he genuinely wonders.

"How are you too? "My brother told me you live in Forest Hill, so I asked for your number for when I was in the area. "I am always around these ends. "This is a cosy little flat still, how much?"

"Thank you. "It's rented. "Should I get you some Supermalt?"

"Nah, I will just share yours. "What's with the big screen? "Are you that blind?"

"Nah, I am not blind. "Wait until you see the next one. "So, your brother knows you are here?"

"Don't worry, he won't chaya you. "I am legal now."

"Legal for what, are you trying to fuck me? "Uh-uh, not again!"

"Where is my gift then?

"I thought you had something for me.

"Give me my gift!"

"Yeah, I do.

"Come here, feel that?"

"Please, stop.

"Not with your dirty dick.

"You haven't showered off your wife's juices yet."

"And you are overdressed.

"What's with all that ass tucked away under that dress?"

"I am a lady.

"Leave my dress alone!"

"You look gorgeous, you've filled out nicely."

"Stop fondling me.

"I will scream."

"Yeah, didn't I tell you, you're to die for?

"The police will have to cut me off you with a chainsaw."

"Seriously, Ollie, get off me.

"I didn't come here for this.

"Put that missile away."

"Wait until you feel the shower," said Ollie, as he continued undressing her.

"Come in here."

"I have already showered.

"You're being silly.

"Your wife will walk in on us."

"You worry too much.

"She will just have to turn and look away until we are done."

"Wow, this is an amazing shower."

"Yeah, Italian."

"As if."

"As if, what?"

"You have never been to Italy, have you?"

"In my head, I have been everywhere."

"Yeah, where else?"

"Close your eyes and I will show you."

"I have been… here."

"Mmm, that's really beautiful.

"Looks just like my tits."

"I don't think so."

"Mmm, those sure do feel like my nipples."

"Nah, I don't remember your nipples being this big."

"They were smaller back then, mmm.

"They sure like you."

"I have also been here."

"Oh, that's a fine long neck you kissed right there."

"You sure?

"I like your neck better."

"Did I show you these jugs already?"

"Aha, those are FFs."

"What about this flat area here, what's this used for?"

"Oh, that? You can caress that.

"That's that good staff called a flat tummy baby."
"You know what I really liked?"
"What's that baby?"
"This little crack here, woo!
"Why is it so slippery and warm here?
"My tongue might just…"
"Oh!
"Oh, jeez!
"Oh, my gosh!
"Oh, you are making me feel dizzy!
"Oh, my jeez!
"Oh, my gosh, baby!
"Keep your tongue right there!
"Oh, that feels so good, oh!
"Oh, my gosh baby!
"Keep your tongue right there!
"Don't stop baby.
"Oh shit, you are fucking amazing.
"Don't stop!
"Oh, I had missed…I had missed you so much.
"Keep going baby!
"Oh, my gosh, oh my gosh!"
"Shush, you are too loud!"
"Shut up baby, just!
"Keep your tongue right there!
"Oh, that feels so good, oh baby!
"Oh, my fucking gosh baby!
"Deep your tongue right in there!
"Oh, don't stop that shit baby.
"That's fucking amazing.
"Oh shit, you are fucking amazing.
"Don't stop!
"Keep going baby!

"Oh, my gosh, oh my gosh!"

"Oh baby, I think… I'm… coming!

"Oh, shit! "Oh, my gosh!

"I'm fucking coming!!!"

"That was a bit loud, you okay?"

"Oh my God, what the fuck was that?"

"That was a squirt baby, remember. "I felt like I was being waterboarded there for a minute."

"Wow, why are you washing my ass."

"Because… I am going to rim, this other door?"

"No, you… can't… "You can't eat.. that… one!

"Oh, my fucking gosh!"

"Shush!"

"Oh my gosh, what are you… doing… to… me!

"Oh, that feels so good, oh!

"Stick it baby.

"Tongue tip that shit.

"Oh my, my fucking gosh

"Oh shit, that is fucking amazing baby!

"Right there, don't stop!

"Keep it right there.

"Oh, my gosh, oh my gosh!"

"Oh shit! "Don't stop! "Keep going baby! "Keep your finger right there! "Oh, my gosh, oh my gosh!" "I'm fucking, coming, again! "Oh, my fucking gosh! Shit, shit, shit! I'm coming!!!"

"Shhh, I'm sorry. "I'm sorry baby. "Was that too intense for you?"

"Oh my God, my heart almost stopped. "Why did you do that to me? "I cannot believe you ate me out like that. "Oh my God, that was amazing! "You guys eat ass too?"

"Well, it needed to be done baby. "Part of your initiation. "Now you know the back door needs just as much attention."

"That was amazing. "I need to breathe, open the window please. "I almost passed-out in here. "Why are you brushing your teeth, are we done, already?"

"Ay, you quit whilst you're ahead, right?"

"Did I come all the way here just to get my pussy and asshole polished?"

"For someone who is supposedly on her period, I must say, I liked swallowing your clear blood."

"So, what, you wanted to give me head while I was on my period?

"You are downright nasty!"

"You need to go, now my lady.

"My wife should be on her way right now."

"What, what about you?

"Look how hard you are, my poor baby.

"Come to mama."

"Another time, seriously!

"She is on her way home, right now.

"Besides, it's disrespectful doing it like this.

"We can't fuck in her house."

"We have already crossed the line baby, it's already done."

They get out of the shower and into the bedroom to get dressed while Nancy continues begging to be pierced by his hot piece of iron. Ollie is fully erect and surely would love to slam that ass, but Deena really is on her way. He will have to finish off with Deena, but Nancy won't give up without trying one last time.

She hops onto the Queen-sized bed and wiggles an ass-clap for him while on all four. Seeing the little pink meat exposed by the arse clap sparks his wires. She sees the look on his face, and she turns over and lies on her back.

"Come to bed baby," she says as she squeezes her own titties. The glistening of her well lubricated pussy and the pink spot slightly exposed underneath her engorged pussy lips catches his eyes as she raises her knees and spreads her legs wide open. "Oh shit, we will go to hell for this shit," he said, as he pounced over her, dicking her out.

"Oh!

"Gently please, been a while!

"Gently please!

"Oh my God, are you suddenly deaf?

"Stop pounding me!

"It's hurting me.

"Please, it fucking hurts!

"Oh

"Oh yes!

"Yeah baby, oh my gosh! "Aww, you are too much! "Slow the fuck down. "It's hurting me."

"Hang on, I'm, "I'm about to, I'm about to come!".

"No don't! "Don't you dare! "Don't you fucking dare. "Not inside me, Ollie! "Pull out, please you can't cum inside me, pull out."

"I'm sorry baby… "I am coming…!"

"Wait! "You're cutting me off! "Wait for me! "You cut me off. "I was about to come too, and you just cut me off. "How could you?"

"Shit! Next time. "Get dressed, quick!"

"Oh, first you fucking shred my pussy, then you cum inside me, cutting me off, and now I must leave? "You better not get me pregnant. "You better pray I don't or it's knee time, again."

"I'm so sorry mama. "I promise you won't get pregnant. "I will pray for you, and I will deliver next time."

"No!

"There won't be a next time,

"Look, you made me bleed, again.

"You premature ejaculator," said Nancy, as she threw the blood-spotted and ejaculate-saturated towel over his head.

"Premature what?

"Bitch, you were busy holding on to me and talking about it hurts, stop, fuck me, pull out, while grabbing my ass.

"You sent me mixed messages woman!"

"Come on, please, where are my keys?"

"You never gave them to me, check your bag."

"I will walk myself to the fucking car, thanks!"

"Don't leave like this mama," Ollie yells as he runs to catch up to her.

"Look Mama, remember last time?

"That's what you do to me baby.

"Look, you are sweet like that.

"It makes me just wanna rush a job, ok?

"I'm sorry. okay?"

"Well, all I remember from last time is it fucking hurting, again.

"If that's how you jack hammer your wife, I wonder how she has stayed with you this long.

"You can't fuck like that.

"Learn to savour the pussy!"

"Baby, I promise.

"We just didn't have enough time for savouring and shit.

"Next time, I promise you!"

Ollie continues calming his mistress down as he walks her to her car. She finally turns and hugs him endearingly and leans in for a passionate kiss. She gets in her car and drives off.

As Ollie looks downhill into the distance, he sees his wife labouring, as she comes up the hill. He stays calm and walks slowly towards her. He is in panic but maintains a sense of calmness. As he leans in for a hug, she shrugs him off leaning away from his face.

"You whore!

"Who was that girl you were kissing?"

"Slow down mama!

"Me, kissing who, where?

"I didn't kiss no one!"

"Fucking liar!

"What do you take me for, blind?"

"Shhh, calm down woman!

"What are you talking about, I kissed who?

"I just sold that girl a passport.

"What, you think I don't have customer service skills?

"She just bought a passport for fuck's sake!

"Let me show you the transfer."

"Don't lie to me, do not try that shit!

"I know what I saw.

"That was not customer service!

"You fucking cheating scam!"

"You know what, you go home with your lying eyes!

"I am out of here.

"See yah."

Ollie's phone is ringing, it's Nancy calling.

"Hey mama."

"Trouble in paradise?"

"What do you mean?"

"Look ahead."

"So, you saw all that?"

"Just enough."

"Enough for what?"

"Come on, homeless man, jump in," she shouts through her lowered driver's window. He gets in and they drive off.

"It's ok my baby, mama's got you.

"She will regret that tomorrow."

"Fucking women!

"One did not get dick the right way and the other did not want the dick to start with."

"Stop feeling sorry for yourself.

"I have a solution to both your problems."

"Yeah, what's that?"

"All you black guys think the dick can solve all your problems, huh.

"What would you do if you didn't have the dick?"

"I would have a big pussy?"

"Stop being such a jerk!

"Use alternatives, like words or gifts.

"Not money, just other gifts.

"Gifts melt a woman's heart.

"Trust me, I am a woman."

"Oh, like I melted your heart back there?"

"You are not even serious.

"Girls are very sensitive.

"Just keep it simple, stupid!"

"How, when it's war out here?"

"Use your kindest words, apologise to her and just persist on that.

"Like you apologised to me and walked me to the car.

"You didn't give up on me even though, just for a minute, I was mad at you for tearing me up, again.

"You persisted until I forgave you."

"Persist, new word."

"Like I persisted and got the dick."

"Yeah, and landed me in a world of trouble.

"I should have just followed my instinct."

"Had you followed your instinct, then you would have missed out on all this to-die-for pussy, right?"

"What's the solution to my other problems then?"

"That's a tough one for you.

"When, and if you ever tap this pussy again, just slowdown from the get-go, some women need slow and gentle strokes boo.

"Leave that jack hammering shit for your wife, if that's what she is into, ok!

"You cannot shred this golden pussy here.

"Baby steps, you understand me?"

"Bitch please, your pussy can probably swallow my whole arm.

"Just shut up and drive!"

"You're just mad right now, but I know you get it!"

"Where are you taking me, why are we here?"

"Chill, you're homeless, this is our home for the night."

"A brothel?

"Besides, who is we?

"Since when have you been homeless?"

"This here is a five-star B&B.

"I cannot leave my baby alone and homeless with all this stress and tension, can I?

"Besides, you owe me, right?"

"Owe you what exactly?"

"Oh, don't get me started.

"You can't just deflower me, be gone for two years and just welcome me back with that half-ass job of yours.

"Should I say more, or just tell Goldie then?"

"I'm still here, aren't I?"

"Good, I am not ready to lose you baby.

"My brother will murk you."

"Yeah right, I will whoop his old ass this time. "I have been training, look at these guns right here. "So, how did you find out about this five-star B&B if all you did was wait for me these past two years?"

"Oh, this here, come inside.

"You will see."

"Oh, I can cum inside now?

"This is not so bad for a broth…"

"B&B, and I own it.

"This here, is my shit."

"No fucking way!"

"Yes way!

"I, Nancy Seke, own this bitch!

"If all you roadman weren't too busy buying expensive cars for your whores, or maybe get refunds, you too would own properties, in England!"

"Ok, my lady, point well taken.

"Just let a brother digest all this pussy juice that's making my belly growl."

"That's just hunger growl.

"I can order you some…"

"Pizza!

"I would like some halal pizza please."

"Ew, carbs!"

"Bitch please, those carbs make excellent dick food.

"How else do you think this dick got so fat?

"It's them carbs.

"You should try them and grow some HH or something"

"Wow, yet you didn't have any problems finding my FFs earlier!

"You know what else, I will be raising you an invoice for staying here tonight, and you're in the doghouse. "Premature ejaculator!"

"Come on mama, you can't take away the milk-milk, please."
"Yes, I can, and I will!
"Order your own goddamn halal pizza, and when you are done, sleep in those jeans too!
"This titty joint is now out of bounds for you!"

Later in the night, while Ollie's phone buzzes the night away, he ignores all Deena's calls and spends an extremely rewarding night with his mistress. With all the distraction from Nancy, Ollie is running critical systems in the background.

He does not allow himself to be pussy-whipped by her to-die-for pussy. While she slowly and gently grinds his dick, he works out angles on how to approach his wife to circumvent pitfalls and land mines with her. He cannot afford to lose Deena, not now, not ever, not for anyone.

On the other hand, he imagines all possible worst-case scenarios with the job ahead, and he is ok with all possible outcomes. He looks back at when he was awaiting his trial in the magistrate court's holding cells, when the lawyer told him how much time he might expect. He realises he was not afraid not because he had gotten numb, he had simply played out the worst-case scenarios too many times and had accepted each possible outcome as fate. The intensity of propulsions this tight, warm and sweet pussy is generating as she comes to another explosive orgasm snaps him back into focus, as they both orgasm at the same time.

Nancy has broken quite a sweat while he drifted into deep thoughts. She smiles at him as she leans in for a kiss.
"You see baby, you finally delivered.
"From zero to hero, whoop-whoop!"

"I told you we didn't have enough time.

"You are definitely official now."

"Official in what way, wifey official?"

"Nah, not yet.

"Official, as in you definitely know how to fuck me.

"Can a brother catch some shut eye now?"

"Let's sleep like this.

"I want it inside me all night, so my pussy can fully stretch.

"I don't want to struggle with it again next time.

"Besides, all that cum inside me will stain my clients' linen."

"Nope, get off me."

"Ok, let's just stay like this a bit longer, please"

"Nope, you're getting addicted.

"I might suffocate in my sleep if these tits choke me for what I said earlier."

"I thought you were gangster, are you scared of titties now?

"Can I at least sleep like this, wrapped up in your big arms?"

"Ok, good night Mama."

"Sleep well baby."

CHAPTER NINE

Deena is at home when Ollie tries unlocking the door, but only she can, her key is in the lock. He was hoping she would be at work but not today. Deena is heartbroken about Ollie's cheating. Had she not seen the towel left on the bed, she would have bought into his story. She would rather turn a blind eye, but how could she with that much evidence.

Had he answered her calls last night perhaps they could have worked something out, but he made a bed and laid in it with Nancy, the same woman with whom he fucked his way into trouble. She has packed his suitcases and all his gadgetry. She has cleansed her house of his infidelity.

Looking at her face, he knows she hasn't slept a wink waiting for him to walk in any minute as he usually did. She is mad at him, fuming at that, but she conceals her pain. She can't even look at him. Every time they make eye contact, she starts weeping.

He sits on the edge of the bed and stays quiet. She is on the other side of the same bed where she sits and listens to the silence too. They are having conversation but only with the angry voices in their heads. Deena finally goes first.

"How is she?"

"She is fine.

"How are you?"

"I mean, how is she at sex?"

"She is alright."

"Was her pussy tighter than mine?"

"What, no!"

"Tell me, how was it different to mine."

"Seriously?"

"As a heart attack, tell me everything."

"We fucked that's all, but I make love to you, you know that."

"Tell me how it led to that.

"How did you end up with your dick in her pussy?

"Don't say she raped you either, I am not playing."

"She, she couldn't leave.

"She had come to get me back."

"Back how, was this a repeat or what?"

"Yes, second time."

"In our bed, you fucked that bitch twice, in our bed.

"How could you?

"What kind of a man are you?

"You fuck random bitches in your wife's bed, how disrespectful?"

"Nah, it wasn't like that. "First time, it was in a hotel. "I was playing for these guys and they booked me a hotel room on the night Caster had asked me to take her along since I had borrowed his car. "I took her there and she literally gave herself to me. "It was all her doing baby, I am sorry, but I don't like her like that. "Every time I fuck her, I imagine it's with you, that's how I get through it baby! "I am attracted to you, I love you please, don't you see that," as he bursts into tears.

Seeing him crying, on his knees and hearing his story, she starts crying too. Some shit a crying man does to a woman. All of a sudden, his tears make every lie he has just told her the absolute truth. She picks him up and cuddles him. He continues snuffling as she helps him dry his eyes. He sits back on the bed then lies on his back, continuously rubbing his eyes.

She undoes his pants and pulls them down, exposing his dick. She mounts onto him and guides his dick onto herself and rides him hard and fast. She groans in intense pleasure as she lets her emotions go. He cums inside her and she collapses on top of him. He nestles her into his arms as she falls asleep on his chest.

When she wakes up from the much-needed afternoon nap, she takes the evidence towel and chucks it in the bin, then starts unpacking his suitcases. For now, he knows he is still in the game, only down but not out.

Deena makes their evening meal which they eat while watching a movie. Knowing her deep thoughting tendencies, Ollie rushes his food just in case shit happens again.

Somewhere during the movie, Deena pauses it and throws him a question that leads to a few others.

"When did you say fucked her the first time again?"

"It was just before we left Godalming."

"We had only just gotten married, how could you?"

"How could you not come with me to my gigs, you know women hit on me!"

"So, you need a babysitter to do your job?"

"Baby, when I met you, was it not at a party?"

"So?"

"So why are you acting like you don't know deejays are hot, you married one did you not?"

"So that's your excuse for whoring around, because I did not protect you from her?"

"No, I am just saying had you been there, it would not have happened."

"But it happened though, you fucked another woman during our honeymoon period.

"Who does that?

"Did you at least use a condom?"

"First time or this time?"

"Both times! Did you protect us?"

"No."

"What if the bitch burns us, better yet get pregnant?"

"She won't burn us, she is clean."

"How do you know she is clean, by fucking her raw?"

"No, she was a virgin."

"You dumb motherfucker, can you hear yourself right now? "What if like you, she fucks raw, anal? "Did you know she can catch diseases that way too?"

"Obviously, I didn't think about that. "You're just mad I fucked someone not only younger than you, but a virgin."

"You are such a jerk; I am done talking to you. "Get out of my house. "Go running back to her. "Get out of my house!"

Ollie had stabilised the ship, had he only managed to quit while he was ahead. He grabs his coat and calls Nancy, who once again, comes to his rescue.

Since the blow out last week, Ollie has been staying with Nancy who is only happy to continue laying with him. Ollie is rejuvenated by her youthful energy and is laying some serious pipe.

Deena has been quiet until now. She has been calling and texting all day, but Ollie has not responded. Nancy finds and deletes the missed calls and texts in typical jealous girlfriend style. By the time she finally gets through to him, she breaks down and cries on the phone and begs him to come back.

Hearing her cry like that breaks his heart. He folds and tells Nancy he is going back to sort things out with her before she hangs herself. Something is off about her; she never cries like that. The fact that she is crying worries him. Deena's manager gives her the week off after she broke down and cried in front of her patients and colleagues.

OLLIE SAVAGE

When she gets home, Ollie is already waiting for her. He has made her favourite dinner. She goes back to questioning him again about Nancy.

"Babe, when I ask you about this girl, it's because I just need closure.

"Can you give me that?"

"Ok, what do you want to know?"

"Are you guys serious, is this us?"

"I wasn't serious until you gave me ample time to get to know her.

"So, I guess we're serious now."

"Is this what she wants, you, me and her?"

"I don't know, I hope it is what she wants."

"Why?"

"Because I am not going to leave you for her."

"Can you just leave her then?"

"So, you can drop me again next week and I am back begging her to take me back?

"Nah, she is my insurance now, she stays."

"Well, if she does, you will be seeing her out there not in my house.

"And you get to sleep in our matrimonial bed every night.

"Can you promise me that, at least?"

"Look, I can't promise you anything right now. "Let's see what happens.

Ollie has continued seeing Nancy on the side but sleeps at home every night. Deena is coming to terms with the fact he may be pairing her up with this Nancy chic. He had always told her that men from his family were polygamous. She had a feeling this might happen one day.

If Ollie is serious about her then she might be the one. She knows if that's the case, she needs to accept it now and come to a fair arrangement. As the first lady, she will make her conditions clear and he has to stick to them.

"So, I have been thinking."

"Ok."

"With you being serious with Nancy and all."

"Uh huh."

"It's not like I never saw this day coming.

"All I want to know is, is this her, the other woman?

"If so, will she be the last one?"

"It's early days."

"I mean, you fuck her well, without condoms.

"Very soon she could be pregnant."

"I haven't thought about that, not yet anyway, she was just an outlet."

"I want to meet her, just me and her, eye to eye.

"Can you give me that?"

"Not sure we are there yet, but I can ask her. "It all depends on how serious she is about me."

"If she is letting you bleed her out in my house, I think she is serious. "Don't you agree?"

"Babe, I really don't know. "Let me talk to her first, she is different. "She can be a bit feisty, let me approach her the way I know she won't feel threatened. "This is a big deal."

"Oh, protecting her now, what do you think I will do, poison the bitch?"

"She ain't no bitch, stop talking about her like that."

"I see, she is special.

"Let me talk to her before I go back to work."

"I will.

"So, you are really pumped about this first lady role?"

"If that's what I have to do then I might as well do it right.

"I mean, your mother did it, and you turned out alright. "So, it cannot kill me, surely."

"It's not plain sailing, my mother suffered a lot of heartbreak.

"I don't think I'm cut out for it though."

"If you are truly your father's son then you sure are cut out for it."

"Thanks for the encouragement."

"In a way, it has its own benefits."

"Like what?"

"I will have free childcare, for life."

"So, will she."

"Nah, I am the first lady, I don't play that shit. "My way or no way at all."

"You will have to play nice with her. Obviously, as the younger woman, she will be highly favoured."

"Nah, you already imagine yourself fucking me when you are with her, that tells me who is your mama.

"Besides, being the younger one, she can look after the both of us when we get older.

"No care home for us, thanks to you."

"Really, you're thinking that far ahead?

"You ought to be ashamed, woman!"

"Seriously though, you hurt my feelings, at least you should have discarded the towel. "Instead, I had to touch her blood and juices, with my bare hands! "You will go to hell for that."

"I'm sorry baby, that was wrong of me."

CHAPTER TEN

Ollie finds comfort in knowing Deena has swallowed her pride and wants to make this work. She truly is exhibiting character traits similar to those of his mother. There are many family traditions and practices in Ollie's family, but being the Englishman that he is becoming, most of them will get lost along the way.

Ollie is adapting, and fast. With a woman like Nancy now taking a greater part of his life, Ollie knows when to make compromises. Hence, he has asked Nancy out on a proper date. Since her comeback, it has all progressed into something too quickly. They sit and wait for their orders in Nando's restaurant.

"So, what's this fancy date all about Ollie, I never saw you as the dating type."

"Well, thanks for the compliment.

"Can a brother not show his wife a good time."

"Wife now huh, is this how you announce my promotion?"

"It's something that's been on my mind.

"I like you a lot Nancy, and I don't think I show it enough."

"Like? as in you like ice cream?"

"Come on, don't burst my balls Nancy, you understand me."

"No, I don't, please rephrase your statement."

"I mean, you are a beautiful, intelligent and loyal woman.

"I like that about you, and I think that's how we have come this far."

"Oh, how about, I am caring, compassionate, sexy, forgiving and amazing in bed?"

"Forgiving, yes. Compassionate, ok. Amazing in bed, now that's all down to me, I think."

"Whatever, you are just a hot body.

"I am the full package, how about that?"

"Oh, so I am just a sperm donor huh, shameless woman."

"Well, a girl has got to eat.

"Look what swallowing you is doing to me," she stands up and gives him a twirl, showing off her curvaceous body.

"Classy, erm, sit down please."

"Why, am I embarrassing you with all this junk baby?"

"No, I get it.

"I am very proud, I tell you."

"You should, because you are one lucky fool to have me," she sits back down.

"About that, do I really have you?"

"Yeah boo, you've got me.

"Are you too blind to see that, unlike you, I don't like you.

"I love you baby.

"Like is how you feel about your shoes or phone, I love you baba."

"Wow, you, you mean that?"

"Yes, I do, should I tell everyone here, will you believe me then?"

"Nah, I get it.

"It's just, I am a serious kind of guy.

"Once I commit, there is no going back.

"So, I ask you, should I commit to you Nancy?"

"I mean, don't get me wrong here but, don't you have a wife already, ain't you already committed to her?

"I get it Ollie, you are that type, the type that wants it all in life.

"Guess what, I respect what you have going on with Deena but, as long as you keep making me feel the way I feel when I am with you, yes you can commit to me."

"Woo, for a minute there I thought here we go."

"Really, am I that unpredictable?"

"Not all the time, you are aiii."

"Look at you, getting your Ali G on.

"You are so funny."

"So, how have you found this whole experience dating a married man and getting involved, putting out the fires?"

"As I said, I love you.

"I just want you to be happy.

"Are you happy now that I am back in your life?"

"I am, and so is Deena."

"No shit, really?

"How?"

"She wants to meet you face to face, just the two of you."

"Is she crazy, what makes her think I am ok with that?"

"Seriously, she wants to meet you and get some shit straight."

"Like what? Give me a heads-up here.

"What if the bitch cuts me or spray acid on me? I don't trust her."

"I do, and she is not a bitch."

"Oh, you gonna defend her?"

"Nah, just reinforcing some respect between you two."

"I don't like disrespect, like, I really hate that shit."

"Oh, are we ok?"

"Yeah."

"So, when does she want to meet?

"Can you set it up?"

"Tomorrow, lunch time, same place?"

"Just pat her down first, make sure she ain't carrying.

"I don't know her like that, just saying."

Ollie really wants the meeting to work so he stays close by and waits in the car watching and listening in from Nancy's phone. It starts off as expected then he hears the two ladies starting to engage more and laughing together.

"Oh my God you are absolutely gorgeous, Nancy."

"Thank you, Deena. So are you, I love your dress."

"Sorry, but it won't fit you."

"God, what a shame. "There I was thinking it makes for an excellent hand me down."

"Oh, don't worry, I can take you shopping another time. "So, thank you for meeting with me."

"Yeah, I had no choice once he started talking in his deep voice."

"Really, he did that with you too? "I hate it when he does that, it's like he is talking to a child."

"Oh, I hate that, but that's how I know he ain't playing."

"Man hey, it's like marrying your father."

"Not sure about that, I never saw my father."

"Oh sorry, what happened?"

"He and my mother split before I was even born, who does that?"

"Oh, shame, same with me.

"My parents split when I was little too."

"Jeez Deena, are we going to cry?"

"Hopefully not, we have so much to talk about."

"Oh, I must tell you, I was nervous about meeting you. "I even asked him to pat you down, just in case you were thinking about, taking a bitch out. "You know, eliminate your competition," they both laugh.

"No, look, I have always known he comes from a polygamous family. "He always told me the stories of growing up surrounded by polygamists and how that shaped up his dream of a big family. "I wasn't going to give him his thirty children all by myself girl," they both laugh

"He wants how many?"

"Nah, just joking. "He wants more, definitely but not that high."

"So, if you knew why didn't you call a bitch quick? I don't mind having his babies, he looks so dangerous yet so adorable."

"Listen to you, sounding all invested.

"Are you?"

"I don't know, I am kind of falling in love with your man Deena, is that ok?"

"Good, now you are talking, tell me everything."

"Like what, are you sure you are ok with this?"

"Bitch please, If I am going to be your first lady then I might as well get all the juicy bits."

"Ooh, first lady, I guess that places me seconds.

"Ok then since you have asked, let's see," Nancy ends her secret call to Ollie as they continue chatting away.

CHAPTER ELEVEN

News has reached Deena's father that she and Ollie had gotten married without his knowledge or blessing. He is furious at Deena, who is freaking out as any daughter loyal to her father should. Her father has ordered her to quit the clandestine marriage and come home.

It's either she follows his order, or she puts Ollie at risk of being hurt. Knowing what lengths her father can go to get his way, she pleads with him to just let her be for once, but to no avail. She tries pleading with Ollie to let her visit him, but he won't hear any of it.

Ollie is not moved one bit by the threats his father in-law is making. He does not think much of him, besides an old toothless dog that can no longer bite. He tries to calm her down, but she has become hysterical and he knows her too well to just go out and leave her to it.

When he sees her like this, he feels helpless. Only this time, it has brought everyone bad memories. Ollie really hates the old man, passionately. Last time they met; he was left feeling like a big fool. He only wanted to marry his daughter, yet he got told he was unworthy, an undesirable son-in-law with nothing to bring to the table.

What hurts him the most was not the level of disrespect, but the lack of appreciation. With most girls being left pregnant these days, here he was being shamed because he has no papers or a reputation on the streets. Ollie has brought Deena some flowers, a card and a box of chocolates. She reads the card, and her heart is torn between these two fighting bulls.

At twenty-four years old you'd think she is old enough to make her own choices, but this old man still has her wrapped around his finger. She pleads with Ollie that he lets her go and visit her parents over the weekend, to explain herself and try to reason with them.

He refuses and bursts into one of his tantrums grabbing her by the throat and slamming her to the wall. She is knocked unconscious and drops to the floor where he beats her up badly, kicking and thumping her. He does not stop going at it until she gets quiet and motionless.

He drags her motionless body by the ankle into the bathroom where he tosses her into the empty bathtub. He takes a few photos of her bloodied body lying in the bathtub. He wants to send him a clear message. He attaches the photos and starts to type, "This is all your faul…"

He does not finish. The sound of Deena's weak and broken voice draws his attention to her. He snaps back to himself again and drops to his knees in panic. He is shocked at how he has lost control of his temper again. The last time this happened was in Godalming and it was just as bad, if not worse.

He is not sure why he had put her in the bathtub. He gets her a wet warm towel and tries to wipe off some of the blood from her fractured nose and busted lips. As he carries her back to the bedroom, he notices a trail of blood droplets dripping from her bottom section.

"Gently, I am in pain," she begs him.

"Shhh, let me take care of you."

"Take care of me, like this baby?"

"I'm so sorry boo, I wasn't myself.

"I lost it again."

"I thought, you loved me, is this what you meant?"

"Don't say that mama, you are hurting my feelings."

"I… thought I had died."

"You almost killed me baby.

"I'm just lucky to still be here."

"Don't say that, I am not like that."

"Until one day you succeed, and you are like that."

"No, no, no, mama, I promise.

"No more one day."

"Well, it's either you or my father, one of you will kill me if you try hard enough."

Deena gets up to take a shower but is unsteady on her feet. Ollie offers her support to walk but she won't let him.

"Call the ambulance. I have a bleed down below, call the ambulance for me please!"

"Ambulance, and say what, you got hit by a car?"

"Anything, just call the fucking ambulance, please!"

"Ok, ok!"

He gets rid of most of the evidence before the paramedics arrive. Had it not been for the vaginal bleeding, she wouldn't have suggested the paramedics, she would have fought on. The paramedics arrive and they have a suspicion for physical abuse.

They discreetly call the police who come to arrest him. He spends the night at the station where he is released in the morning. They cannot charge him with anything since Deena will not press any charges. She claims she was mugged.

He follows her to the hospital where she stayed the night while they monitored her vaginal bleeding. She has not picked up any of her father's calls to avoid escalating the situation. Ollie feels rotten to the core as he watches her hooked up to all these monitoring machines. He promises himself he is done smacking her. He hates taking after his father.

The doctor in charge comes in with a positive pregnancy result. He tells them she is about six weeks pregnant, and she could have lost the baby had the bleeding gotten any worse. For now, she is ready to get discharged and go home for some rest.

The doctor asks to have a word with Ollie.
"Seriously man, are you a wife beater?
"Am I looking at a big scary wife beater right now?"
"What are you talking about?
"You don't know me!"
"Don't be such a loser, if you don't love her then leave before you kill her!
"This is not how to love someone!
"Get out of here, man!"

Ollie knows he has been caught out. Someone else out there knows he almost took her life. How could she have been pregnant, he wonders. The fertility clinic told them it could take up to six months before she got pregnant when they took out her implant.

The realisation that she might have lost the baby or her life shocks him to the core. He has been looking forward to his first legitimate child since Bonny. How could it happen like this? Was this the child's way of making themself be known? Well, they sure are aware now.

Ollie knows Deena's most recent misfortune was a close call. He elects to move out of the house, arguing that he is a danger to both Deena and the pregnancy. He vows he will continue his husbandly duties but from outside. His presence here stops her family from visiting and raises unnecessary risks.

If this happens again, he can hurt Deena, or the baby and he cannot bear that thought. He promises her, he does not ever want to be like his father. Deena insists he stays but seeks professional help with his temper.

The next day, she agrees to call her father and lets him know that she is with all the family she needs and if he has a problem with that, then he does not deserve her. He stays silent and Deena ends the call. She has taken some time off from work so she can fully recover.

Ollie is her baby. She feels he just needs the right amount of love and he can be a really good husband. She sees a lot of potential in him and with the right motivation, he can be someone powerful one day. She is also very attracted to the danger and unpredictability he brings. She feels fragile and vulnerable around him. That shit excites her.

Nancy has been feeling emotional and burnt out, so she has asked Ollie to come over. Ollie has brought her flowers, a card and some colour therapy books. She is over the moon about the colour therapy books.

She feels it's exactly what she needs as she has been a bit emotional and cranky with her brothers lately. Ollie rips the pack and lets her try them out. She goes quiet for a moment as she concentrates on her colouring.

"This is amazing baba; I feel calm already.

"I swear I was gonna rape you today with the way I was feeling.

"This has really saved your life," she looks at him smiling.

"Rape me, what's up with that, are you ok?"

"Yeah, sometimes I just miss you.

"I hate that about you sometimes, but then, it's what makes me love you so much.

"That feeling of I have you, but I can't have you, if it makes sense.

"When you are not here I want you, when you are here, I want to keep you all to myself."

"Right, having daddy issues again are we?"

"Nah, come on, take me seriously!

"Don't you see I miss you?"

"You don't 'miss me - miss me', you worry about losing me."

"That too perhaps, but I want to sleep with you in our bed, like you have it with Deena.

"I want that for us, feeling your naked warm body next to me.

"It's much more therapeutic than this kiddy colouring shit." She throws the colouring book into the bin as she bursts into tears.

"You don't love me.

"Why are you not here with me if you really love me?

"What does Deena have that I don't, huh?

"I suck good, I fuck good and I drive you everywhere!

"When do I get to be your first lady?

"Is this the life that besieges me now?

"I fucking hate this!" She hugs him, resting her head on his shoulder with tear drops soaking up his shirt. He knows this is out of character, even for Nancy, and as such, he wants to investigate.

"Grab your keys, let's go to Tesco and grab some dinner," he says as he grabs her waist from behind, pushing her out of the door. He grabs a basket and picks up a few microwavable dinner items and a three-set pregnancy test kit. They get home and enjoy a meal together but Nancy rushes to the toilet twice for a sicky. He has seen all he needed to see.

When she sits down he tells her she is pregnant. She doesn't believe it. Ollie reaches into his jacket's pocket and hands her the test kits just to be sure. As she comes out of the toilet, it's obvious to Ollie the mounting days have paid off.

"I hope I am not pregnant; I cannot be pregnant.

"I am not ready to be a mother, I have too many things to do before I have children, babe.

"If I am pregnant, this is on you, this is all your fault mister!" as she sits down next to him afraid to reveal the results. Ollie takes them off her hands, checks all three and breaks a smile. "Congratulations my love, you are not," he pauses before continuing again, "getting away with fucking this fertile man that easily."

Her face lights up but quickly goes back to crying.

"Oh, my mother will kill me for this. I promised her I would not be following in my sisters' footsteps, yet here I am, nineteen and pregnant!

"I can't go through with this Ollie, I can't!" she continues crying. Ollie knows these are just hormones raging through her body. Everything she is feeling is new and frightening to her, all her feelings are elevated. He grabs her, surrounding her with his arms. She needs to know he has her back at this very moment. This is crucial to the survival of his offspring. If the panic sets in, she may elect to terminate. So, Ollie lets Deena know what's happening and she asks to speak with her.

"Hello Deena."

"Hey Nancy, how are you boo?"

"Deena, I am so sorry, I got pregnant."

"That's ok darling, congratulations."

"I don't know Deena, how am I supposed to feel?"

"Exactly how you are feeling now, I've got you darling, I will look after you, ok?"

"You'd do that after everything?"

"I know you'd do the same for me, do not be afraid ok.

"I am pregnant too and it feels amazing once you get past the shock darling."

"You too, how far gone?"

104

"Just two months, I was just as shocked as you are when I found out."

"But you guys are married, what were you afraid of?"

"Long story, just come over ok, and we can talk all about it, ok?"

"Are you sure I can come back to your house, after everything?"

"Yes Nancy, just come over it's fine, see you soon ok?"

"Thank you Deena, really, thank you. "Bye."

It has really surprised Ollie how well Deena has taken to her role as first lady. Since she invited Nancy over, all Nancy talks about is how Deena is such an angel. She feels she couldn't have done it without her.

She had given abortion a thought but, only while under the influence of nerves, once Deena calmed her down and reassured her that she is in good company, she was very happy to have met with her that day in Nando's. With the two women now secure with each other and their pregnancies, it is time for Ollie to play his part as lover and provider.

CHAPTER TWELVE

While Deena is on her placements, Ollie is hard at work recruiting the most promising bikers. For this massive smash and grab project to work, he needs disposable people. People he will never feel bad for not visiting, if they go to jail. He needs sheep, people who can fall in line. He needs a bigger team, a lot of extras, for diversion.

Lastly, he needs plates, underground parking without CCTV, burners, getaway tube routes and a buyer for these goods. The job itself is not too big as it's a three-man job tops, if they want to get caught. For this reason, he needs lots of extras, insured bikes, valid MOT, tax, communication channels, cash payments and has a firm grasp on his team to minimise risk.

It has taken some doing but Ollie is keen to see it through. With all the details finally wrapped up, its rock and roll time. Midday is the best time since shutters are open and most people are having lunch. There are very few shoppers in the way, less collateral that way.

There are some twenty odd bikers altogether, there is more distraction than needed, but Ollie believes in better to have and not need. The core team rides up to the front of the shop and parks. They quickly rush into the shop with their harmers out and secures the eight customers and two staff.

The business owner is surprisingly submissive, he stays calm and cooperative. He tells his customers to remain calm so no one gets hurt.

The security lads are guarding the captives very closely, no one makes a move. The hammerman smash up all the glass and force open the locked cabinets, while Ollie and two other men bag the goods. They only take what's within reach and leave without entering the back.

Ollie radios the extras who arrive outside raving and popping wheelies, further causing panic and distracting the gathering crowd. The rest of the core crew rush outside and make a spread getaway. Ollie notices one of his two men has split with some of the goods and gone his own way, clearly ignoring his orders.

Ollie and the other man ride into the underground car park nearby where they take their kits off and load the bikes and bags of goods into the rented van that Caster is driving. Caster is off, and so is Ollie and the help, who takes his payment and disappears into the busy central London crowds and takes the tube.

After securing the goods, Ollie and Caster track down the runaway man using the trackers Ollie had sewn into the kits he had tailor made for them. They have found his gps location, which leads them to a house on the corner of a street in Brixton. They sit in the car and wait for it to get dark.

The goods must be in there, wonders Ollie, as this is not the address he had given him. The mobile number Ollie had is no longer live, he must have thrown away the sim hoping he would not be found. Lights go on and off in different rooms, so there has to be at least one person in the house. Now that they know where the guy is, Ollie and Caster need to devise a plan to get their goods back.

Ollie and Caster have been hanging around Brixton following the seizure of their goods by one of Ollie's men. They have confirmed his residence and have not seen anyone else but him going in and out of there. Tonight, they ambush him and recover their goods. As it gets darker, they lay back in the car behind the tinted glass.

Caster has brought in a bottle of fuel, Ollie is not keen on doing stupid shit, but to avoid unsettling Caster, he leaves him to his devices. The coast is clear, it's 'go time'. As they creep up to the house, they hear booming bass from loud music. They split as Ollie takes the back while Caster takes the front door.

As Caster knocks at the front door, no one answers. Ollie is nervous as fuck. He has never taken a loaded piece to a job, but knowing what's at stake, he takes in deep breaths and stays calm. Caster breaks the door glass and turns the latch from inside, opening the front door. As he gets in, he meets Ollie in the hallway, and they both sweep the house.

They find no one downstairs but hear some faint footsteps upstairs. When they get upstairs and sweep the rooms, there is no one either. As they are taking a closer look again, they hear loud footsteps coming from the attic. They find the opened hatch and await his return.

The young man from the attic finally comes down the dropdown ladder and surprise-surprise, he is already wearing one of the watches. Ollie tags him with a right hook knocking him out on his feet. He falls hard, his head bouncing off the laminated floor.

Ollie checks his pulse and guards him while Caster climbs up the attic where he finds tons of other stolen gear but only takes what they are owed. He gets down, drops the bag down and click, bang! Caster puts one in the back of his head. He feels disrespected and enraged. He pulls out the small bottle of petrol from his hoodie and asks Ollie to do the honours, he was one of his men after all.

OLLIE SAVAGE

Even though this was not part of Ollie's plan, he obliges knowing the man could not get any deader. Ollie douses him in petrol, then all the rooms before lighting it up. As the house sets ablaze, they drive off knowing full well the other guys will get the message.

The original registration plates are replaced, and the van is cleaned and returned to the hire company after a week. It's a clean job that has brought a big yield, but for now, they are stuck with the goods and murder on their conscience. Your average businessman has not heard of this brand of watches, let alone the people in Ollie and Caster's circles.

All Ollie knows is, whenever he sells one of these watches, he literally becomes a filthy rich man. For now, he can only keep them away from Deena. She will not have hot goods in her house, she believes he is finally clean and knows way too much to be his enemy if she flips.

When Ollie planned to stalk their watch thief, he clearly told Caster not to do any stupid shit that could send police or some wannabe gangsters their way. Caster breached his trust by blowing the kid's brains out right in front of him. Ollie did not want the kid dead; he is not that rotten.

He has been dealing with the nightmares ever since the incident. Every time he falls asleep, the incident flashes before him. Sleeping next to his pregnant wife Deena, he is heard talking to the kid in his sleep, apologising over and over.

When she asks him in the morning, he claims he has no recollection of talking in his sleep or apologising to anyone. Nancy has heard him sleep talking as well, only this time, she has recorded him on her phone. Upon waking, she plays him the audio. Clear as day, Ollie has been visited by the kid again.

109

"Hey Kiddo, how is the land of the dead?
"I am sorry it had to go down that way kid, why did you let greed come between us?
"You were a good kid, I trusted you.
"But you know my hands are clean, I didn't pull that trigger.
"That was not my bullet kid.
"You know who shot you, he was right there.
"Forgive me kid, forgive me.
"I planned the jump; it was my fault I led him to you.
"Sorry kid, please forgive me, so we both find peace."

Faced with that recording. Nancy pleads with Ollie to tell her everything or she walks, and he will never see her or be a part of her life again. Based on the evidence, Nancy knows whatever this is, Ollie did not do it. Someone else was with him and whoever that someone is, they have blood on their hands.

In a bid to gain his trust, Ollie finally curves in and tells Nancy everything. Finding out it was her brother, who had killed some kid does not seem to surprise her, but rather disappoints her. It turns out this was not the first time. Caster had been to prison for another murder but got away with accessory due to insufficient evidence.

Nancy pleads with Ollie to not get involved with Caster as he might end up going away. "Caster is dumb and reckless; he is not smart like you. "You need to run your own shit, or he will drag you down with him," she warns him. Ollie promises he will branch out and do his own stuff, but Nancy takes it one step further.

She tells Deena as he had refused to tell her himself. Deena had a suspicion but could not force him to confess. Unlike young Nancy, Deena does not sweat him. She lets him be, until he tells her in his own time. The nightmares continue to haunt him until he finally confesses to Deena.

CHAPTER THIRTEEN

Ollie is reporting at Electric House again today. It's the same procedure except today, he is issued with an ARC identity card. He feels good about this, it feels like his case is going somewhere. The new shiny card is a minor distraction, he quickly remembers why he feels like shopping today. He goes into a tech shop and has a feel of what's out there.

He is impressed with how far technology has come. He feels as if he has been asleep for some ten odd years that time passed him by. He buys some music software, a gaming computer, a seventy-five-inch 4K tv, some high-end card printers and some burner phones. He gets into a taxi and gets home before Deena returns from work. When Deena walks in, she is astounded by the transformed house.

"Hey baby.

"What's with the studio?"

"I thought you were done with music?"

"Hey mama.

"You know I am nothing without my music babe.

"It's upgrade time."

"Oh, and who paid for all this?"

"You are looking at him."

"I thought, we couldn't afford this, what's changed?"

"You worry about money too much," as he gives her a big hug.

"Give me some sugar."

After an excellent attempt from Deena to replicate a Master Chef dish, they both tuck in and go over their day. He finishes putting away the clean dishes and hands Deena a game console and teaches her how to play FIFA.

She smiles as she knows even though he hasn't got much, he is trying. Out of the blue, Deena asks what Ollie's dream job

112

is knowing everything he knows now, to which he responds, "criminal advisor." Deena laughs so hard that she pees herself.

She can't believe how funny he can be sometimes. She wonders how he can sit there with a straight face and say that without giving it much thought. She takes it as a very silly joke and moves on to whinge about her mentor who had never worked with her but still went on to fail her.

Whoever said student nurses had it easy was surely misinformed. If only Ollie could count the number of times they consummated just to make her feel better about her day. He treats her work-related stress as a good thing because it only means more for him. When she is feeling like this, she likes her doggy fast, hard and deep.

There are advantages of living in a big block of flats like this, too many people already come in and out. So, when Ollie's work from home business takes off, there is zero suspicion. He has gone back to his old ways, only better.

He is processing cheques, IDs, driving licences and work permits. The influx of European immigrants who can't speak English means more people without the right papers, which in turn drives demand for his services up and Ollie is only happy to supply.

The laws have changed, but so has technology. Ollie's prints are of the highest quality. Without verifying with the right bodies, you will believe your own eyes. How is his work different to any other fraudster? He hires graphic designer students who surely appreciate the rates he is paying.

Ollie believes everyone has a price. Selling your soul is easier than one might think. It all comes down to the right offer to compromise one's integrity. These students would much rather make a grand drafting some logo than flip burgers for minimum wage. For Ollie, he would rather pay a grand to some kid he can control for one logo that he can use countless times.

Immigration is big business and with lesser risk. Nobody gets killed, Ollie does not want blood on his hands. If the people finally get caught, they play ignorant, 'I don't know this'. Worst case scenario, they are put on a plane back to Albania. It's a safe and steady income for Ollie who only works on recommendations.

He gets another stream of income from the employment agencies who are paying him for finding them these hard-working people. They, on the other hand, get paid in cash, tax free by farmers who do not wish to pay the alternative rates. He is making his money now while he can. The government is closing in on these dodgy employers.

An even bigger stream of income just came in today. Caster is making too much money shipping cloned cars to Zambani. He needs someone to do his VIN numbers. Ollie is the only person he knows who has tech like that. He will pay a grand a pop.

Given Zambani's political sanctions, the government is bitter and will not allow any western governments to interfere in their internal affairs. As such, any money, goods or services arriving in the country is their property; they will not allow any of it to be touched or examined by foreign entities.

With all the connections Caster has, Ollie is kept on his toes with prints and arranging shipments. He is more involved than he anticipated. The more involved he is, the more money he makes. Caster is not that much into tec, simple things like sending a fax vex him. He likes Ollie's loyalty; they have worked together exceptionally well over the years and he knows too much to double cross.

Every time a new opportunity comes, Ollie heavily invests in the tech to go with it. With the Albanian market slowing down, it gives him more time to focus on the big money. The 3D printer is paying dividends with Caster's cloning business. Apart from VINs, he also needs plates and service histories.

Since Deena completed her adult nursing graduating with a first-class Honours, she has since secured a full-time job at St George's Hospital in Tooting, where she did her placements. The baby is due in a few months. Since Ollie cannot legitimately purchase a house outright, he gives Deena the ten percent deposit needed to secure a mortgage.

Her credit profile and a new job allows the banks to trust her with their money for a bigger property. They settle for a deluxe three-bed house opposite their rented flat, alleviating some of Ollie's storage issues. Now he has his own dedicated office for the music studio and another for the heavy printing gear.

Reporting to the home office has become the norm for Ollie. The money stacking problem has been resolved. He washes his money through betting shops where he places bets on guaranteed winners. The winnings are transferred to different bank accounts. The banks see gambling money and they leave it at that. To avoid falling victim to the Proceeds of Crime Act, Ollie sends most of his money back home, where it's protected, and money transfer agencies love the business he brings.

A letter for Ollie has come through the post. He has been allocated a case worker to handle his asylum application. In it, are a few important details and an appointment with Zoe, the case worker. He is over the moon and reaches out to both Deena and Nancy who are ecstatic about the news.

Nancy's brother, Goldie, is now on board and happy with the arrangement between Ollie and his sister. All Deena wants is for Ollie to be a man and take care of business at home and not to ever abandon any of his other children for her sake.

It's the day of Ollie's first appointment with Zoe. Nancy drops him off at the office's entrance for his appointment and goes home where she awaits his call with updates. Zoe assures him that legal aid is just as good as lawyers at preparing his case and that her firm will do everything in their power to make sure he has every chance to get a win.

They spend the afternoon going over all the critical information but there is missing evidence to support his case. He is asked to bring his supporting evidence to the next meeting so that they can submit the complete package to the Home Office.

Seeing the opportunity that lies ahead, Deena finally convinces Ollie to apply for college. She has found out that asylum seekers can get enrolled into college for a reduced fee, as long as they have evidence that they are in receipt of NASS support. He welcomes the idea but will have to see after he has carried out his own research.

Lambeth College has offered him a place to study for a level three access to biosciences course if he can pass their aptitude test. He passes the assessment and is enrolled on to the access course.

Deena has elected to spend some time with Nancy who has been complaining of lower abdominal pain. She thinks the sort of pain she has been describing is more than the stretching of the womb as the foetus grows. They are attending her booked appointment at Lewisham hospital, South East London.

She is checked in by the midwives and asked to take a seat. Nancy had been reluctant to know the sex of her first pregnancy, opting to leave it as a surprise for her man until now. When she is finally called up to be seen by the doctor, she asks Deena to come in with her.

They look at each other as the doctor rubs the cold jelly on her tummy. Seeing her exposed big tummy, Deena can't believe how fast Nancy has grown. Compared with her much smaller bump, she feels Nancy might be in a world of pain if she gets too heavy too quickly.

As the scanner starts sending the black and white images to the screen, the doctor turns to her and smiles. She smiles too but unaware of what he sees. "Congratulations mum, you are carrying twins," he says, printing copies for her to take home.

"You see here, you have two sacks clearly divided in the middle. One in each sack, classic example of unidentical twins. Now, if you look here, and here, you are carrying unidentical twin boys. Well done. Congratulations mum," he said, wiping some of the jell off his hands.

Deena and Nancy both cannot believe it. "That's why you have been in pain mum, your womb is expanding too quickly to accommodate the twins. "You are absolutely fine, you can go home now, eat healthy, drink lots of fluids and just wait."

Nancy and Deena have both been fighting for Ollie's attention and rightfully so. During these tough times, they are both just getting to understand pregnancy and the hormones that are contributing to their behaviour. Ollie had seen it all growing up. He has developed a thick skin for it, splitting his time equally to appease both women.

He attends most if not all their doctors' appointments and takes them shopping whenever he has time. He cannot allow them to feel neglected at these crucial times of their lives if he wants them to ever get pregnant again. The risk of either one of these women getting her womb sown off due to a bad first pregnancy is very high.

During their routine check-ups, both Deena and Nancy's pregnancies have flagged up preeclampsia and gestational hypertension respectively. There is something definitely in the water. Ollie is trying to make sure they eat healthy, but the pregnancy cravings push these first timers to order takeaways and throw away the rubbish when Ollie is away. He tries to intimidate the local takeaways to not serve them any of their junk food but to no success.

Due to early complications, Deena has taken maternity leave since she had been struggling with her balance which saw her tumbling over a few times putting her and the baby at risk. Nancy too has slowed down from her B&B business.

Ollie and Caster elect to manage it due to her hip pain induced by the heavy load. All baby preparation gear has been stacked up, mostly coming from Ollie and Nancy's brothers. Nancy's mother has welcomed the wonderful news of her pregnancy and is fully supportive of her daughter.

Deena has not been in touch with her father since he refused to acknowledge her marriage. She is now talking to her mother who she never got to know, as she was raised by the different women in her father's life.

She has been in touch with her younger sister, but she still has not removed the sanctions barring her from visiting their house. With Deena now past the seven months milestone, she is no longer panicking about an early delivery as predicted by the doctors. She feels her baby is fully formed now, so every day that passes is a bonus, since she only needs to put on a bit of weight now.

Nancy's check-up has revealed that her gestational hypertension has only gotten worse. She has clearly not been following the doctor's advice to eat healthy and stay away from the salt. Ollie is confident he can help her by making her regular meals that she can freeze and defrost when she is ready to eat. He has also bought her a blood pressure machine so she can keep a close eye on her blood pressure.

CHAPTER FOURTEEN

As if Ollie hasn't got enough on his plate already, he and Deena welcome their first child, a beautiful baby girl who is delivered by caesarean section. Both mum and baby are healthy and should soon be up and running.

In the meanwhile, Ollie helps with mum's showers and housework as well as his daughter's needs. They make it work until mum is back on her feet. They have fallen in love with the baby so much so, all is forgiven and forgotten. The only thing that matters is their family's health and wellbeing. Until Nancy's twin pregnancy proves problematic that is.

Nancy has been lurking in the shadows while the focus was on Deena's pregnancy. The doctors believe her twins may not go full term due to gestational hypertension. The key now is to eat healthy, avoid high sodium foods and get plenty of some tender love and care. College is proving too much for Ollie, who had not seen a classroom since leaving his village aged sixteen.

It is a shock to the system waking up to a crying-hungry baby, a five o'clock alarm and catching the packed train which drops him off where he still needs to walk in the rain and snow the rest of the way. Hope is not all lost as he gets a day off on Wednesdays to report at the Home Office and squeeze in some side-hustle, assignments and baby mamas' time.

He has finally submitted all the supporting evidence for his case and Zoe has assured him that he has one of the best cases she has ever worked on. She is confident that this unique case only leads to refugee status. He takes copies of transcripts from Zoe and goes over them while sitting at the back of the 197 double decker bus that he had missed.

He writes a short poem reflecting on his journey since arriving in England. Reading it back to himself feels as if someone else had written it. It's only at this very moment he realises he is truly talented at something. He doesn't finish admiring his own work when his phone starts ringing.

"Hello, Ollie here."

"Congratulations baba.

"How is my grand-daughter?"

"Mother, how are you?

"Your grand-daughter is very well.

"Oh, she is so beautiful mama.

"How are you feeling now?"

"You know me son, I don't die easily.

"You will have to put up with me for quite some time.

"How are my daughters-in-law?"

"They are both doing well, mama.

"Just trying to keep them from killing each other, but we are all well otherwise."

"So, you heard about the pacemaker, right?"

"I heard mama.

"I think you know where I stand with that.

"I feel it's too risky given your age.

"There are infections especially, to worry about and it won't guarantee immortality mama."

"I know my son.

"I have told your siblings, but you know them, they just want you to sponsor everything.

"Personally, I feel that I have lived my life long enough.

"I am happy taking my chances with the heart God has given me."

"Aww, thank you mama.

"I am really glad you feel that way too.

"How is my boy, Bonny?"

"He is all grown up now.

"He is at school right now.

"His mother came by yesterday.

"She is doing well for herself."

"Thank you, mama.

"Tell him, I will bring him over once I have my papers mama.

"Anyway, I will talk to everyone and make sure they understand."

"Take care son, and remember…"

"There is an opportunity in every situation, I know mama.

"I am learning on the job."

"Love you baba."

"Love you more mama."

Ollie has a bond with his mother even after all these many years apart. He last saw both his parents in the village before leaving for England. Now he only sees them in pictures or memories. He is a real mama's boy, seen as he is the youngest of eight. His mother does not see the youngest, she sees the reasonable one, the most responsible child and her best creation. He has the last word when it comes to his mother's wishes.

He believes they are tied at hearts due to their ability to feel each other's emotions. Being the most important woman in his life, Ollie is committed to looking after his mother, giving her all she desires. Hence, he told both Deena and Nancy, he was already married before they met him, to his mother. That way, they both know their place in his life.

As Ollie checks in with Nancy, he finds her making dinner with the help of brothers Caster and Goldie in the kitchen. They say their welcome greetings and make space for the couple to catch up.

"Hey mama, how have you been?"

"I have been busy as you can see, I cannot lie down, these boys still need someone to feed them."

"Shouldn't you be the one being taken care of?"

"How can I? Their women keep leaving them.

"They just don't want to grow up, so that's my life now."

"Look, you need to put you first, babe."

"They are helping you know?"

"Don't get worked up, I'm only looking out for you and this heavy baggage you're carrying."

"I will stop getting worked up if you stay in here and help me instead."

"First things first, I need to check your blood pressure.

"Where is the bloody machine?"

"Bloody machine?

"Is that what they are teaching you in college, doctor?

"It's called a sphygmomanometer, and it's in the lounge."

"Can you get it for me, your brothers are sitting in there."

"Oh, are you scared?

"Just take the steak knife, no one will touch you baby."

"You are being a dick.

"They will start a conversation with me if I go in there.

"Do you want to cook by yourself?"

"I smell Chicken."

"I am no chicken.

"Look," as he shouts out, "Yoh, Goldie, bring me the sphygonorrhoea thingy."

Goldie brings the machine over and reiterates, "It's called a sphyg-moma-nometer".

"Knee time," yells Nancy, to which Goldie shrugs as he walks back to the lounge.

"It's still in the box Nancy!

"It's never been used, really?

"So, I bought this so it can gather dust?"

"Stop with the yelling, you will wake up my babies!"

"You all are so ignorant; God help me not choke a bitch up in here!"

"Choke who?

"You will not leave this house alive dummy!

"Play that silly shit over there, at Deena's house!

"We are thugs over here!"

"Sit your fat-ass down, you ignorant…" he doesn't finish his sentence as Nancy looks him dead in the eyes. She doesn't like people using profanity around the kids on board. She sits on the kitchen stool allowing her heart rate to return to its resting state.

As the reading is displayed, there is shock and panic in the room as it is way higher than the last time she was seen by her doctor. They check it again, and again until it is clear that she has a bad case of gestational hypertension. Ollie calls the ambulance which takes the expecting couple to Lewisham hospital after confirming their worry.

While on the way, the emergency responders put dopplers on Nancy to monitor the babies' heart rates. Their heart rates are not good, twin one has a very high heart rate whereas twin two has a much weaker one. They inform the couple this only means the twins are struggling but will have to hand them over to the specialist doctors on arrival.

They are checked in to the maternity ward where they are seen by the doctor on duty and the midwives. Her urine sample flags up preeclampsia. The dopplers indicate that twin two's heart rate keeps dropping. At twenty-nine weeks, the twins are just about fully formed but are way tiny.

The doctor orders a caesarean section and Nancy is immediately injected with a steroid to help with the urgent development of the twins' lungs as part of her preparation for surgery. Everything is happening too quickly, Ollie has not had time to notify Deena or Nancy's brothers about what's happening.

The doctor has informed them about everything that can go wrong with these pre-terms' health ranging from developing lung and breathing complications, infant diabetes and even death. Caster and Goldie arrive and await updates in the waiting area.

The midwives inform them she is being prepared for surgery as the babies are no longer safe in her belly, they are in distress but will only have to wait. Ollie is dressed up in scrubs for health and safety. He holds on to Nancy's hand as he comforts his woman.

They are both not comfortable receiving an epidural from a trainee doctor. They try to talk their way out of it, pleading with the observing and much more experienced doctor, but it lands on deaf ears. She tightly squeezes Ollie's hand as she receives the epidural from the trainee doctor. It has been administered safely and it's a go.

The surgeon starts cutting along the dotted line on the fold between her lower belly and pubic bone. It is gruesome to watch for Ollie, he looks away and holds on to Nancy's hand for support. "Suction please, irrigation, forceps, scalpel, irrigation, suction," is all Ollie hears repeatedly as the surgeon proceeds. Nancy is so numb from the epidural she can't feel any of the slicing and hacking that's being done to her.

After what seemed like an hour, they finally got twin one out. His umbilical cord is clamped and cut. The suction tube is shoved into his mouth and nose, clearing his airways.

He is wrapped up and placed under some light heater. The surgeon starts tagging on twin two's tiny leg.

For some reason, he is stuck. The surgeon is working as fast as he can, every second counts. It's intense, Ollie is worried but hangs on to Nancy who is in and out of consciousness. The last thing she mumbled was, "I feel very cold."

The theatre staff are keeping their eyes on the job. The surgeon cuts, irrigates and sucks one last time and untangles the umbilical code from twin two's little neck then yanks him out. He looks blue, and motionless.

His umbilical cord is clamped and cut. The suction tube is shoved into his mouth and nose clearing his airways as well. He is wrapped up and placed under the same light, next to his brother. They are taken away, not sure where, for now. The attention is on mum.

Her heart rate is dropping, oxygen saturation down at eighty nine percent with the oxygen mask on. She is quickly cleaned up and stitched back together. She is covered in warm blankets to stabilise her. The surgeon is done here, the surgery was a success on his part.

"Congratulations mum and dad. The twins need a lot of medical help, I am sure you have been briefed. Mum, you will feel much better very soon. You are in shock. Just get warmed up and you should be able to see your babies in the neonate."
"Thank you doctor," says Ollie and Nancy at the same time. It is a big relief for this lucky couple.
"I want to hold my babies Ollie, where are my babies?"
"Why didn't they let me hold my babies?" queried Nancy as she is wheeled by one of the nurses to the recovery ward.
"We will be seeing them shortly, I am sure.

"You heard the Surgeon; they need a lot of medical support.
"Just get better mama."
"I am better already; I want to see my babies please."

The nurse leaves her in her cubicle and assures Nancy she is off to find her babies and will be right back with information. True to her word, she comes back after the longest quarter of an hour they have ever endured and tells them, the twins are stable and just being checked and closely monitored by the neonate staff. They can now see them. They follow the nurse to the lift which takes them to the neonate floor.

They walk towards the two little incubation tanks housing their tiny twins. There is tiny and there is this, the mice sized babies. Twin one weighed in at a thousand kilograms and twin two weighed in at a mere eight hundred kilograms. Seeing the sheer size of the babies, the wiring hooked up to their noses, veins and the masks on their little heads, Ollie's heart just sinks.

He feels they do not stand a chance. He has already painted a worst-case scenario in his head. To him, he has already lost his babies, there is no way they will live. They are just way underdeveloped. Twin two's face is not fully formed, the nose looks a bit funny. Ollie is hurting.

Nancy looks at her babies and breaks a smile, she separately places her palms over their separate incubators and starts praying for them. When she is finished, she introduces herself to them.
"Hey babies, hello.
"I am mama.
"I have been waiting so long to meet you.
"I have brought baba too, okay, he is here.
"He is just a bit emotional right now, ok?

"We both love you, so much, ok."

Seeing Nancy smiling and talking to her babies, Ollie's heart starts beating again. The fear of losing the twins is relieved. He has just found his strength in Nancy. He too, places his palms on the glass incubators and welcomes his babies into the world. Tears of relief run down his cheeks and Nancy passionately and discretely wipes them off. She gets the reassurance that his heart is in this.

The doctor comes over and greets them. He goes over an exhaustive list of possible defects the twins might develop due to their development stage, size, weight and response to their new environment. He also reassures them that the twins are in the best of hands and they will be closely monitored until they are safe to go home. This does not phase Nancy one bit but worries Ollie who has college in the morning.

Day one saw the twins getting delivered with an oxygen deficit, especially twin two. Their assigned doctor hooked them up to quite a few cables through the nose, belly button, feet and hands. They kept drawing blood for all these never-ending tests. Tests for red blood cells count, tests for inherited diseases and a brain scan to see if there was a concern for Down's syndrome. By day two, most of the results were either in or the tests needed to be redone for absolute confirmation of their findings.

As Ollie and Nancy watch on, they can't help but wonder where all the blood is coming from given the sheer size of their babies. By the end of day two, the doctor informs the couple that both their babies may need blood transfusions as the initial tests have shown lower RBC count.

If the babies' bone marrow does not kick in and start blood production, they may not make it past day four as they are already just getting by. On the morning of day three, tests reveal their bone marrow is not producing any new RBCs as the numbers are actually going down. This means either their bone marrow is not fully developed or it's taking a bit longer to activate.

The Muslim in Ollie pleads with them to wait until the morning of day four to check again, since he does not believe in blood transfusions. Nancy just wants her babies alive and is willing to give her own heart so they can live. No one is allowed to visit the babies at this stage. Both Ollie and Nancy do not want anyone seeing their babies like this, except for Deena.

They are just too tiny and surrounded by too much wiring and tubing. By day four, the brain scans have revealed some good news, their brains are fully formed and there is no chance of developing Down's syndrome. It's quite a relief.

Not long after celebrating the brain development news, they are given some bad news, the RBC counts have not improved. With the lower RBC counts, the twins are at risk of developing anaemia, shortness of breath and organ damage due to a lower oxygen delivery. Ollie curves in and the twins receive their first blood transfusion.

Having pleaded with his God to allow his twins to live, he now understands the importance of a blood transfusion at this critical stage. So, when the choice rested with him to either allow his twins to live or die, he chose life. Everything else simply had to wait. When Nancy asked him why he finally allowed the transfusion to be carried out, Ollie replied, "I'd rather take my babies home alive."

By day five, the twins needed some more blood transfusions as they were still not producing their own RBCs. Same as day six and seven. By day eight, they stopped receiving blood. Their bone marrow was now fully functional. Their oxygen dependency had reduced significantly.

The doctor was gradually reducing the volume of oxygen they were receiving. Most of the wiring and tubing was also reducing. By the end of week two, they only had a nose feeding tube, heart rate and pulse monitors and getting weaned off the oxygen.

During the twins' hospital stay, Ollie and Nancy were visiting every day. Ollie would visit in the evening after college, while Nancy was in and out all day expressing and delivering their breast milk. The nursing staff had to stop her from bringing in more milk in the end.

She was producing so much milk, filling their freezer with just her own milk. She opted to donate whatever she did not need, as there were other babies who were not getting any or enough from their mothers.

Time soon flew by once they had started receiving mum's milk and were growing. Their little bodies started filling out and their funny looking faces started looking cute. Finally, Nancy was allowed to breastfeed her tiny munchkins.

Everyone was kept well up to speed as Nancy had created a social media group that she was constantly updating with pictures and videos. After two months, they were finally welcomed home by a big crowd from both Ollie and Nancy's families, including Nancy's mother. The twins' home coming party was truly special.

With all his babies now in their respective homes and thriving, Ollie has some unfinished business with college and the Home Office. He is on track to finishing college with more distinctions than required for entry into the university of Surrey.

The only barrier in his way is that his settlement has not been decided. The legal aid company that was handling his file went into administration, leaving Ollie's file to be passed on to another firm. This is really bad news for Ollie and could not have come at any worst timing. There is not enough time, with only three months left before Ollie starts university in September.

Ollie has not completely given up on his university plans. He has lost the fire that once consumed his heart about becoming a doctor. His father hasn't got long, he is dying of prostate cancer and he cannot help besides calling and sending money for his medical bills. His mother is constantly in and out of hospital with fall injuries, hybrid diseases resulting from her hypertension and diabetes combo.

Will he ever catch a break, he wonders? Everything that could go wrong is still going wrong since he set foot in England. It has all been downhill from there. He is starting to feel as if it's karma, he is being punished for his hand in all the bad things that are happening in the world.

He has received a letter stating that he has been allocated a new caseworker with another firm in Birmingham. They go over the details over the phone as the new aid Jaimie, feels the case has no substance. He feels Ollie's case is weak and has a lot of holes that they will use to deny him his potential refugee status.

Jaimie is no kiss-ass. He has too many cases to go through and his firm gets paid win or lose. He advises Ollie to withdraw and restart a new application. Ollie feels as if this will take forever. He has a sneaky feeling these guys just want to spend as much time on his case, so they get paid for the hours.

However, he tells Deena about the new development and she wants to know if the file can be sent back so they can take a closer look at it for themselves. Deena is smart, as long as it's written in a language she understands, she can figure something out. Ollie is hopeful.

The big file is delivered and signed for, both Ollie and Deena go over it and they cannot see anything wrong with it. They send it back to Jaimie with the instruction to submit it the way it is. Jaimie agrees but informs Ollie he will have to accept their decision once they have denied him the right to stay in the UK.

It is worrying on Ollie's mind. Keeping his ears on the ground, he knows the Home Office is getting strict with asylum seekers. Most are just claiming asylum as a means to buy time while still working illegally. A few church friends have been deported and their bishop has been kept on his toes visiting them in removal centres offering prayers.

As September comes to pass, Ollie has neither gotten an appointment with the Home Office nor started university. He is told that they can defer him until next year but nothing more than that. With his place for university safe until the next academic year, Ollie has time to focus on his expecting wife and everything else.

Babysitting has been resolved as Nancy and Deena have found common ground. They take turns babysitting their children when Deena is at work and on her days off. Ollie spends most of his days working on his side hustle and helping Nancy with the children.

Deena's father has pleaded with Ollie that they include him in his granddaughter's life. He has let bygones be bygones and has now accepted Ollie and Deena's marriage. Deena is hopeful that the grandchildren will really help mend her relationship with her father. She is willing to move closer to him so he can help them with childcare due to her constant falling out with Nancy.

She hates fighting with her in front of their children and feels now is the best time to make the move before the next baby arrives. Ollie is not too keen on the idea as it's too risky. There is no guarantee that this arrangement will be any better than what they already have.

Ollie's business is booming but he has to restart all over again. He has raised enough money to secure another mortgage for another three-bedroom terraced house in Gillingham, Kent. Nancy feels abandoned to fend for herself with the twins. Ollie pleads with her to be patient and reassures her he is working on a much bigger plan, but for now, he needs to set everything in motion. She is not happy, but she trusts him and believes his every word.

With the distance so much further, Ollie has been allowed to report at Electric House once a month as he has never breached his terms. The time he takes on the long journey from Gillingham to Croydon is the one time he gets to plan his future goals and endeavours. The journey feels shorter than it is.

While he is in London he spends his day with Nancy and the twins, learning the business of B&Bs. Nancy has bought another property that she is developing and encourages Ollie to get on to the property ladder once he has his papers sorted.

"How are you so sure my love, that I can do all that?"

"Why not, everyone could buy a house if they saved enough.

"Once you have saved enough for a deposit, the property pays for itself.

"All you have to do is pick a good location with either students or tourists."

"So, is that your business model then, exploiting innocent students and tourists?"

"Exploiting, me?"

"No, I just know how to invest."

"What is the most challenging thing about your brothel business?"

"B&B!

"You call it a brothel business one more time!"

"Sorry, I went by that word for a very long time.

"I just associate B&Bs with whore houses.

"Haven't you heard?"

"Well, do you see any whores around here?"

"Well, times have changed, but do you honestly think all these couples coming here are married?

"Accessory to prostitution if you ask me.

"Just saying."

"Well, you hold on to that medieval way of thinking and you'll die a BBM."

"BBM?"

"Broke black man, you've never heard that terminology?"

"Nah.

"You know, for someone who has never set foot on a university campus, I must admit, your English is very good.

"Better than mine, in fact."

"That's because you are a village boy.

"Did you speak English in your little N'ongwa village?

"I went to school with white kids, do you think we all spoke Chinga?"

"Point taken."

"Damn, I'm good.

"Another one to me."

"I don't know what it is about your cutthroat ways, but it kind of turns me on."

"Am I supposed to be afraid of you, like Deena?

"I am not afraid of you, I am with you because, somehow, I am attracted to you."

"And Deena is not?"

"She is afraid of you leaving her, that woman.

"Maybe she needs a man to feel complete, I don't.

"I want a man to love and respect me the way I am.

"As long as you keep doing that, you'll have a purpose in my life."

"Why me though, when you could have chosen anyone else?"

"I don't know, maybe I liked the bad boy in you.

"You are like my brothers in a way, and you know us girls, we either marry our fathers or our brothers.

"It's what we know.

"You were a familiar type of bad."

"And now, how have I changed?"

"That's the problem, you have not.

"I thought we would be going to the movies together, shopping every day and going to church every Sunday but, no, not you.

"You had to be married to Deena.

"How could you not see me, when I was here for your taking all that time?"

"Come on, leave her out of this.

"I see you, alright.

"How do you think we made those two babies?

"I don't know, you jackhammered me while I was ovulating."

"Stop messing about, I am serious.

"I see you mama; I just love you both."

"Nah, you see, love doesn't work like that.

"You can only fall in love once."

"That may be, but who said anything about falling in love?

"I remember saying I love you both."

"Oh, okay.

"Let me ask you then; are you in love with me?"

"Yes."

"Are you in love with Deena?"

"No."

"Really, then why are you still with her and not me, the woman you are in love with?"

"Why does everything have to be either or with you?

"How about you answer this.

"Did you know I was married when we first met?"

"Yes."

"Did you think I would leave my wife for you?"

"I don't remember, that was a long time ago."

"Ok, how about when you came back, in Forest Hill.

"Did you know I was still married?"

"Yes."

"So, you came into another woman's house and fucked her husband in her bed, what was that?"

"Look, I was horny as fuck, and I didn't care.

"I just wanted you back."

"Did you think I would leave my wife for you then?"

"I don't know.

"Are you having regrets we created those most beautiful babies in the world then?"

"I am not regretting that.

"I am just showing you how complex love is.

"The same way you love your twins equally is the same way I love you, Deena, every one of my children and more."

"Every one of your children, how many have you got?"

"Just one more.

"I have another boy, Bonny.

"My first son with my high school sweetheart.

"And Deena is pregnant, probably another girl."

"I think I have heard enough.

"But how did she get pregnant so soon?

"Is she dumb?

"Doesn't she know about contraceptives?

She is supposed to be a nurse!

"No words!"

"That's the first."

"First time you are telling me the truth, for sure! "So, this kid is in Africa, right?"

"Don't worry, he won't be a bother to you."

"Yeah?

"Will you bring him over?"

"Only if you want me to."

"Of course not.

"Are you still together?"

"No, it was a one off."

"Yeah, you have a real gift with one off knock ups."

"I'm sorry, can we talk about something we are both passionate about?"

"Babies!

"So, when do you expect to knock me up again."

"Is it a race?"

"I don't know.

"You over there giving your wife ample time to catch up to me, so why should I let that happen.

"Come on, fuck me before my babies wake up."

"No.

"Stop it, Nancy!"

"Why?

"Did you stop Deena from climbing that pole?

"You are here now.

"Might as well do me, right?"

"That's not how I want to do this.

"The last time I fucked you, you had twins.

"I want to make love to you next time, slowly, make love to some soft music, so you can have a singleton."

"Oh, I can't wait.

"Look, all that dirty talk about babies just got my knickers all wet.

"I am drenched already.

"Give me that bad boy!"

"This is rape, just so you know.

"I have not consented to this.

"This is rape!"

"Yeah, then why are you grabbing my ass?"

"Am I?

"I have no choice.

"I just want you to get off me."

"Why is my nipple in your mouth?"

"I am just checking to see if the children are not drinking poison.

"I just want all this to stop."

"Knock me up again!"

"Not again, no!

"Please stop now!"

"Yeah, you are making me drippy with that talk.

"Keep begging me to stop, baby!"

"Stop, it hurts.

"You are hurting me.

"You are bending my dick the wrong way.

"Stop soaking me up with your wet pussy!

"Please get off me.

"I won't come back here again."
"Oh, don't stop!
"Keep going baby.
"You are making me want to explode all over you.
"Oh, there it comes.
"Here I go.
"Are you ready!
"Oh, my gosh I am coming!
"I am coming.
"Oh, oh I am coming."
"Shhh, you are waking them up.
"Gently.
"There you go.
"Just ride it out.
"Just like that, well done.
"Are you ok baby?
"Is it all out?"
"Aha, oh my God!
"That dirty talk was amazing.
"Did I offend you baby?"
"No, that was hot, but you cut me off."
"Really?
"Then why does my pussy feel full of your cum?
"If I get off, I will spill it all over you.
"I need a towel."
"Use my t-shirt."
"Oh, thank you boo.
"Mmm, letting me wipe with your t-shirt.
"I will have to wash it now, so you cannot leave just yet."
"You were soaking wet, are you sure you are not ovulating?"
"And if I am?"
"Good, because you might be looking at nine months without salty foods."

"That would be like a prison sentence.

"I love my salty roasts."

"You almost killed my babies last time."

"Well now we have something in common."

"How so?"

"You almost killed Deena, twice."

"I was stupid, what's your excuse?"

"I was ignorant."

"Yeah, that's what worries me."

"How?"

"How are two people, who are admittedly ignorant and stupid, allowed to create life. "I don't get that. "What kind of children are we bringing into this world?"

"Why is your phone on silent?"

"Leave it!"

"Deena is calling you and you're ignoring her; she knows you are busy hammering my sweet pussy."

"The less she knows the better, trust me."

"So, if one of the babies wasn't feeling well and I called you while hammering Deena, you wouldn't answer my calls?"

"And say what, I am being raped?"

"Just answer her, please, for me."

"You answer her."

"Ok," as she gladly answers the call.

"Hi Deena."

"Hi Nancy, are you with my husband again?"

"Yes, he had stopped by to donate, but he is all done now.

"Hold on," as she passes the phone to Ollie who takes the phone and walks out-side through the rear double doors.

"Hi mama,

"How are you doing?"

"Just finished work.

"Do you need a lift home, to our house?"

"Nah I will catch the train; I bought a return ticket.

"I cannot spend another hour with this woman, she talks too much.

"I might just choke her."

"In that case, wait for me.

"I should be just over an hour," she hangs up.

Nancy sees Ollie's face and says, "Don't let her guilt you up.

"She wants you back, doesn't she?"

"Nah, she is coming to fuck you up."

Ollie enjoys these talks with Nancy, not just for the added benefit, but he finds her easier to talk to than with Deena. When it comes to matters concerning his children, she simply shuts him out.

As the superior woman in their entanglement, she should be approachable. She should be the one keeping the other women in line. However, Ollie knows she has his back when it comes to other matters concerning his welfare. It's possible that she cannot handle it all. They both have a special place in his big heart.

Since moving to Gillingham, there have been confrontations between Ollie and Deena's father, coming to blows. Ollie feels that he has tried everything to earn his father in law's respect, but he has failed. He has done everything in his power to show him that he loves and respects his daughter.

However, his father-in-law sees failure in him. He constantly reminds him of his poor upbringing, how he never accepted Ollie because he could not provide for his daughter. He is simply too poor to earn his respect.

141

OLLIE SAVAGE

He went as far as wishing his application falls through so he can get deported back to the village where he belongs. This was when Ollie lost it. He had let him go too far for too long.

He caught him with a straight right, flash on the chin, knocking him out cold on his feet, then dragged him out of his house, tossing him out onto the street. When he staggered back onto his feet, he warned Ollie to watch his back as that was not going to be the end of it.

When Deena heard what had happened and asked Ollie about it, he blatantly denied it. Saying if that had been true, then he should have called the police on him. Seeing as his daughter had stayed with her husband, he took it as dishonour and stopped contact with his daughter. Ollie and Deena had no one else around them but each other. This brought them even closer. Ollie stopped his side hustle and concentrated on raising his children.

Ollie and Deena are shocked to learn of her father's passing. Kent police are treating his death as suspicious, since pulling out his body from the River Medway with a gunshot wound to the chest. They promise to do everything in their power to find his murderers who they believe are still out there.

As they leave, they give them a contact card in case they think of any information that can help the police with their investigation. Deena is devastated and heartbroken so much that she won't even eat, bath or take any consolation phone calls. Ollie is left with the task of looking after her and their daughter. He asks Linda to come and stay with them for a while as preparations for his funeral are underway.

They finally get his body released to them for burial. It's a big turn out as most of his estranged children and baby mothers have attended to see him off. Linda has decided to stay on for a while longer, as Deena has taken his death personally.

She almost gets to blows with Ollie, after accusing him of murdering her beloved father. Ollie tells her that they had their disagreements but that's as far as it went but she is convinced he either killed him or had him killed. Linda cannot take the fighting anymore, so she leaves them to it.

When Ollie finally received a letter inviting him for an interview in Solihull, West midlands. It was a much-awaited break as he had waited too long and had been worried he might be taken in one of their infamous dawn raids and be forced on to a plane without a fair trial.

As the days drew closer, Ollie was getting more and more anxious, wondering what the outcome would be. If all goes well, he will soon get his papers and confirm his start date with the university. If everything goes pear-shaped, he will receive a letter from the Home Office's immigration department simply giving him a limited time to say his goodbyes before getting kicked out of the country.

The later was not an option. Ollie would fight tooth and nail to be removed from his family. With both Deena and Nancy aware of the two possible outcomes, they arrange for childcare so they can both accompany him on the two-hour drive to the centre where the interview is taking place.

Upon arrival, they are told that the visitors cannot be accommodated at the centre while the interview is conducted. Ollie goes through the airport-like security, repeatedly being searched by the guards and scanned by the body scanners. By the time he passes through the third and final check, he is exhausted by the level of security and wonders if they have decided to just skip the interview altogether.

The interview is running thirty minutes late. The interview is now running forty minutes late, Ollie notices as every second strikes away on the big wall clock. With all his belongings held in a locker by the security, he feels he is at their mercy. He is tucked away in a pocket of uncertainty. There are no warranties or choices here. Once you are in here, you cannot change your mind. The only way out is if someone lets you.

"Mr Nevanji, this way please," says the lady who will be chairing the interview.

"Please take a seat."

"Thank you."

"Did anyone come with you today?"

"Yes, my wife."

"I am sorry we kept you waiting."

"Are you well, and in good health?"

"Yes Ma'am."

"Please don't call me Ma'am, I am not that old yet, thank you."

"I am so sorry."

"Right, can you confirm your details please.

"Starting with your name, date of birth and address."

"Oliver Nevanji."

"Are you right or left-handed?"

"Right-handed."

"Can you sign here, here, and here please."

Ollie signs.

"Right, are you happy to start your interview?"

"Yes, I am."

"Will you start by telling me when you arrived in the UK?"

"December 24th, 1999."

"Can you tell me which port of entry you used?"

"Heathrow airport."

"What was the reason for your visit?"

"Visiting family."

"How long was your entry clearance?"

"I don't follow."

"How long was your visa, the one that was stamped in your passport?"

"Fourteen days."

"Why did you stay on after your visa expired?"

"My guardian had plans to renew it."

"But it wasn't, was it?"

"It was renewed but it turned out it was not genuine."

"Never renewed then?"

"Yes Ma'am."

"I told you to stop referring to me as Ma'am, did I not?"

"I am terribly sorry.

"Please do not let that affect your decision making."

"Why did you seek asylum and not apply for a spouse visa?

"It says here your spouse is British, correct?"

"Correct.

"I didn't want a spouse visa."

"Why not?"

"I am not with her for her papers."

"Did you know about the option to apply for a spouse visa?"

"Yes."

"So why seek asylum?"

"I am at risk of being persecuted if I return to my country."

"Mr Nevanji, persecution is a strong word.

"Do you understand the implications of what you are telling me here?

"Must I remind you that the answers you give me are going on record.

"Do you understand that?"

"Yes."

"So, who wants to persecute you?"

"The Zambanian government."

"That is a very broad statement.

"Do you have any specific people who are after you?"
"The President and his officials."
"When did you become aware of this plot to persecute you?"
"When they set fire to my village, burning women and children because of our religion."
"When was this?"
"About eight years ago."
"Do you have any dates and time?"
"It started on the 3rd of April 2001."
"That was nine years ago.
"Why did you not seek asylum back then, why wait almost ten years?"
"I genuinely thought I had an indefinite leave to remain here.
"I thought it would not affect me.
"I felt safe as I was already settled here.
"That's why."
"That doesn't answer why you did not go back to your country before your visa expired, does it?"
"I do not understand this."
"Mr Nevanji, when did you get the fake visa in your passport?"
"In 2004."
"So, if that's true, why did you not go back to your country before the village was burnt?
"There is over a four-year gap in which you could have gone back to your country, if you wanted to."
"There are two reasons.
"After I left the village, my father informed me that it was not safe for me to return as there was a civil war there, incited by the president's Christian supporters.
"Secondly, my guardian had already submitted my passport for a visa renewal.
"Either way, I could not travel."

"So, if all your family was mercilessly murdered and wiped out, how did you find out about the details of their deaths?"
"They did not kill everyone in my village, only the Muslim families including mine."
"That does not answer my question.
"How did you find out about the details of your family's massacre?"
"Through my friends who I was still in contact with."
"What's your friends' names?
"Do you have their contact details?
"Can they confirm all this?"
"I am sure they are all married and have left the village now for better lives.
"I have lost all contact with them.
"After finding out my family was mercilessly wiped off the face of the planet, I lost hope.
"I gave up on that life.
"That's why I never set foot there again, I had nothing to return to."
"So, do you know if they ever got a proper burial?"
"From my understanding, they have a way of doing things like that.
"I heard they were buried by bulldozers in a mass burial," he tells her, as he wipes tears off his face.
"I am sorry Mr Nevanji.
"I know this must bring back really distasteful memories.
"Would you like to take a break?"
"Don't mind me please, I always cry every time this comes up.
"A whole clan of people, now only two left, my sister and I, and our children," he bursts into full on crying."
"Mr Nevanji, please come here.
"Let me give you a hug.

"You have sucked the breath out of me with your story.

"Please stop crying, I think I have everything I need.

"Here, have some tissues.

"I am so sorry for bringing all that up.

"Let's take a break," says the interviewer, as she wipes tears off her face.

It seems at this point the break was well timed. When the interviewer comes back, she has a very gentle approach.

"Mr Nevanji, thank you so much for putting up with all the questions.

"Please understand that I have no bad feelings towards you or your people, I am simply following protocol, ok?"

"I understand.

"Please forgive me.

"I didn't know it was still such a sensitive subject.

"I honestly thought I was done mourning my people."

"Ok, Mr Nevanji.

"It says here you are in college.

"What are you studying?"

"I have finished my access course. I was meant to start my biomedical science studies last September, but we are here."

"I am so sorry to hear that.

"What made you want to study biomedical science, that's quite hard, is it not?"

"I wanted to study medicine so I could treat my mother's hypertension.

"After they were...

"I saw no point in pursuing medicine.

"Biomedical science is my passion.

"I love the science of life," looking to the ceiling as he held the tears back.

"I understand.

"Listen to me, Mr Nevanji, I wish all the people who come to this country were a lot like you.

"It is people like you that we seek to help.

"I know it's tough going through the asylum process, but be rest assured I will do everything in my power, to make sure you get a fair decision.

"I cannot make you any false promises, but just know that you have walked the longer part of your journey to get here.

"No more reporting at Electric House for now.

"Our decision will now determine what happens to you, ok?"

"Thank you, Ma'am."

"Not Ma'am, but from you, I will accept, ok?

"That concludes our interview Mr Nevanji.

"Can I see you out now?"

"Yes please."

"Have a safe journey home now and good luck," she says, as she walks him through to security.

As soon as he comes through the main entrance, he dials Deena's number, courtesy to the first lady of course.

"Hey baby," answers Nancy.

"What are you doing with her phone?"

"Oh, I have her handbag.

"Are you done with the interview?"

"Is that my husband?" shouts Deena from the background.

"Love you too babe, wait for Deena," she says, passing the phone to Deena.

"Hey baby."

"Oh my God, you ladies sound exactly the same.

"I am done, where are you?"

"Uh, shopping.

"How did it go?"

"Can we just go now, please"

"Nancy, talk to your man, he wants to go home, now."

"Hey baby, can you come into town, towards that big roundabout with the MacDonald's on the left.
"Just turn right from your direction and come to the mall, we are in Debenhams," she hangs up.

"Fucking women and their shopping, now I have to walk," he talks to himself. Nancy has taken the role of classic bad cop. Ollie goes over the interview questions as he walks the short distance into town. He is critiquing every answer he gave, and he is not pleased at all. He feels he should have practiced better.

It is no longer in his hands, the decision never was in his hands, but the hands of those who have power over his destiny. He notices the smiles on his women's faces as he approaches them. They do not look ready to leave. It's already been an emotionally draining day for him. He just wants to get home and bends over either one of them.

To his surprise, the clothes and shoes are not theirs but something they are doing for him. Something to cheer him up with. He is pleased that they have found something they both have in common. They both enjoy dressing him up but they both have very different tastes in his clothing.

Deena prefers the lighter colours, white, blues and khakis whereas Nancy is all black. Black t-shirts, jeans and shoes. He ends up cracking jokes with them and playing romance the rest of the afternoon and on the long drive home. Not at any one point did anyone address the elephant in the room. It ended up being the best day no one had ever hoped for.

Over the next few days Nancy is spending more time at the Gillingham residence. She starts cooking and sleeping over. She gets her own air mattress as day trips turn into a week's stay. They spend more time talking about his likes and dislikes, in life and in bed, until Nancy reveals to Deena, she is carrying another set of twins, one of each.

Deena takes it to heart and starts avoiding Nancy. Nancy gets it, but instead of confronting her, she gives her time to deal with her own pregnancy. Ollie does what needs to get done and simultaneously plays the romance card with both of them.

CHAPTER FIFTEEN

Six weeks ago, on this very day, Ollie was sitting in a very emotional interview in which he shared a tear or two and ended up snuggling up with a stranger. A lot has happened since then. The women have since become friends, then frenemies, then back to uncertainty again, as each day passes without knowing what fate awaits both their born and unborn children.

All Ollie knows for sure is, if he gets removed from the country, then it will take some doing as his whole clan is coming with him. There should be enough to replace the ones that perished in the village fire. So, you should understand his reluctance to wait for Deena before opening the suspicious looking letter that he signed for this morning. It has come from his representing law firm.

"Dear Mr Oliver Nevanji

Following your interview with the Home Office dated 24/06/10, we hereby write to inform you of the developments that have taken place following…"*Just get to the juicy part.*"

"Congratulations…
"Granted refugee status…
"Five years..
"After which you can apply for an indefinite leave to remain. We will forward to you all the paperwork once received from...

Since our work here is done…

"Yours since…"

"Oh my God," he shouts loudly.

"Unbelievable God."

"Only you my Lord," as he dials Deena's phone.

"You have reached my voicemail… beep!"

"I can't breathe," as he dials Nancy's phone.

"Hey Babe, what's up?"

"Oh, my goodness babe."

"What, what happened?"

"Guess."

"You have won the lottery?"

"No."

"Don't call me at that loud profile to play 'guessing games' with me, spit it out."

"I got it!"

"It what? Spit it out!

"Stop playing with me!"

"I got my refugee status baby!"

"Yay!

"Hooray!

"Holidays, whoop-whoop!"

"Who is that? "What's going on Nancy?" Deena interrupts from the background.

"Hold on for Deena," as she passes the phone to Deena.

"What's with the hollering baba, and how are you telling her first? "What is it?"

"Babe, I got my refugee status."

"What, just like that?"

"Just like that baby.

"I just received a letter from that Birmingham law firm.

"They will forward the documents once they have received them from the Home Office.

"This is it baby, no more worrying, this is it."

"Congratulations baba.

"Let me talk to Nancy and see if we can come over.
"Give us two minutes," as she hangs up.

Ollie calls his sister Gloria to share with her the wonderful news. Gloria is over the moon for her younger brother. It has taken him quite a few years to fully appreciate this day. Now he truly understands what it means to earn the right to be in England. As the famous British saying goes, 'it is a privilege to be granted permission to live here'.

He runs to the door full of vigour, like a child, to help his women and children into the house. This calls for celebrations. It's feasting time as Nancy helps Deena set the table for a big Nando's dinner. They feast and talk about their future dreams; a big family holiday is number one on their list.

Since getting his papers, Ollie has been busy applying for a few entitlements. At the start of the academic year in September, Ollie feels blessed to be at the University of Surrey. It is one of the top ten universities in the UK.

The fact that he has made it here speaks volumes. He is academically astute, just like any of the other students in his group. They have all come from different walks of life but with one common goal, to graduate first class. How many will achieve that goal, it's anyone's guess.

During the first week, introductions are underway. Students are getting to know one another; tutors and professors are getting to know their students and the students getting a taste of what they are in for. By the end of week two, they have mostly settled in and naturally paired up based on their common interests or physical attractions. The coupling has already begun. As Ollie and other mature students know, some of these early couples will fizzle out while some will go on to have children or get married.

By week four they receive their first assignments and it's time to bite down and graft. First year is not that intense, it's time to bring all the students up to speed. They have all come from different academic backgrounds so year one is just levelling up. It is simply repetition for Ollie and some students with 'A' levels.

For those without a sound science background, Ollie elects to help out, therefore establishing his dominance. He wants them to know there is always help at hand but implicitly, to let them know he is boss. Slowly and gradually, the course intensifies, and more help is needed. Some students are lagging, simply due to the lack of confidence or a poor level of English.

With more work piling up, Ollie encourages them to do as much as they can for themselves, so he only helps with grammar. Some of the students simply lack the time to do assignments. They need to take extra shifts, so they can send money to their respective countries, while some need to raise the steep international students' fees. If only Caster knew, he wonders.

One by one they ask for help completing their assignments. They offer cash and gifts in return. With rent money as Ollie's only source of income since getting his papers, he sees an opportunity to make an easy buck. He picks his marks wisely, turning down high-risk students.

He takes money from the smart kids he is confident in, the catch is they have to at least read the assignments, so they know the level of detail required. As time goes by, he gets new students and loses others, some are one offs, and some are long term.

The grading system is simple, get over seventy percent and you are in first class. The assignments credits are put towards exam credits and the average is your score. As long as they do not completely fold in the exam, they are safe.

Some of these kids are just spoiled. They come from homes where mummy or daddy spoon fed them all their lives. They never had to step up and get what's theirs in the big bad world. A perfect example is Lynx, he feels superior, above everyone else. Lanky, tattooed and perhaps handsome to these first-year young women.

These girls drool over him. He shows up when he wants to, never participates in lectures, he is alright-ish in practicals. One of Ollie's regular clients, Sally, has mentioned him a few times. She has been seeing him on and off, but he won't be seen with her on campus. Apparently, he wants to keep his options open.

It has caught Lynx's attention that Sally is nailing her assignments, so he asks her for help with his. His excuse, he is too busy. When he offers her coke and money as payment, she comes clean. She finally introduces him to Ollie, the man behind the top marks.

Ollie does not like the kid from the get-go, he feels Lynx has that 'entitled to shit mentality' whereas Ollie has worked his ass off to get here. This lazy kid somehow rubs him off the wrong way. He does not seem afraid of him or at least show some level of respect.

"Hey Pal, Lynx." He says, as he remains standing, nodding at Ollie. Sally grabs one of the two empty chairs and sits down. "Do you want to sit?" She asks him, noticing introductions going wrong. This kid is jittery and has no street code in his bones. Instead of asking for a seat like a gentleman, he stirs down at Ollie who is loudly typing away on his MacBook.

He always sits in this corner of the cafeteria when he is working. No one evades his space unless it's really full.
Ollie looks up at him and then looks at Sally, as if to say, 'check your boy'.
"Can you sit down, please," she pleads with him.
"Oh, I'm sorry," said Lynx.
"Lynx, this is Ollie, the guy I was telling you about.
"Ollie this is Lynx, the guy I always talk about."
"Nice to meet you, Lord Lynx," he continues typing away.
"Nice.
"Are you too busy or something?"
"Nope, Why?"
"Sally can you please, let us talk?"
"Sure, see you later, Ollie, Lynx."
"Is that your bird?"
"Nah, just some chic."
"So, you won't mind sharing then?"
"Sharing, nah, all yours Pal."
"Ollie, please."
"Sorry, Ollie, and you can have her."
"You talk like a boss man.
"What's up, am I picking up the right vibe?"
"Me, nah.
"I am no boss, just a commoner, like yourself."

'Commoner', Ollie sits up and looks deep into Lynx's eyes but he looks down. He has had this 'commoner' term used by some English aristocrats on some history tv show. He takes a moment to not feel judged or deliberately provoked. He assesses that the kid in front of him is certainly no 'commoner'.

He dresses too well, blending in but still standing out. Going by his choice of wording, sense of fashion and bullish attitude, he susses out this kid must either be a drug dealer or some type of old money. No 'regular Joe' has all these qualities tucked up under one collar. He digs deeper.

"So, what's a commoner like you doing, asking for my help?"

"I haven't asked for anything yet, have I?"

"It's the chair my man, it's the chair. "People only sit in that chair when they are ready to submit themselves to me.

"Are you submitting yourself to me, Arthur Buchanan?"

"Well, if you put it that way, nah.

"I will see you around, Pal"

"You'll be back Arthur!"

"Whatever!"

He tucks his hands into his leatherjacket's pockets, as he walks away. He gave away some crucial information to Ollie. He is a very proud young man. He is a boss, and definitely not the commoner imposter he wants to be.

He refused to second himself to Ollie, for now, which is exactly the reaction Ollie was looking for. Now he knows who he is dealing with. There is competition for territory on this campus, it's only right he learns more about his opponent and what's at stake. For now, Ollie concentrates on delivering his five-star service.

Word has reached Ollie that his father has finally passed away. The battle with prostate cancer has finally got the better of him. With end of year exams looming, it is bad timing. Ollie cannot attend his father's funeral, not because of exams alone, but due to his refugee status. He can never visit his country using his refugee's travel document. It is tempting but he has his priorities set.

He buys Gloria a return ticket who flies out to see him off. It is a big funeral, every living member of the family has come to see him off, wishing him well in the next life. Videos of the masses singing and dancing to their traditional drum uplifts his spirit. Aged eighty, his father finally gets laid to rest. All his wives are in attendance standing on each side of his grave as they lower his cascade.

It is an emotional scene for Ollie. Last time he saw his father, he was handsome, strong and working hard on his land. He knew nothing else besides growing vegetables, breeding livestock and looking after his big polygamist family.

As the first lady of House Nevanji, his mother will continue looking after his every son, daughter and grandchild. Even though she is old and frail herself, she will continue to love, support and advise, passing on her knowledge to the many grandchildren and great grandchildren. For now, it's goodbye Baba, may your soul rest in peace.

CHAPTER SIXTEEN

Deena is back on maternity leave. She has given birth to another beautiful baby girl. Coming from a long history of girls, Deena has come to terms with the fact she may never give him a male heir. Unlike his forefathers before him, Ollie does not care much about the sex of the child.

With the many step siblings, cousins and nephews Ollie has back home, he can care less about the village chief's throne they're fighting over. Nancy, however, due to another bout of gestational hypertension, has prematurely delivered another set of twins by c-section. A bouncy boy and girl this time, bringing her total to four. With Ollie's women now best of friends, on and off, childbearing has become a friendly battle.

With Nancy's upper hand with the boys and overall numbers, Deena prides herself in quality over quantity, bearing only a special breed of people, girls. The pressure is on both parties to catch up to the other. With business going so well, Nancy has no intentions of trying her hand at anything else, besides giving her man the greatest gift of life.

Deena on the other hand has been feeling a bit depressed and can't wait to get back to work. She wants to move up the bands as most people she graduated with are now band sixes and she is still a band five. She feels she is better qualified than most of her band six sisters who knows extraordinarily little about critical care. Ollie being the supportive husband, always encourages her to apply for band six jobs.

Today is car shopping for Deena. Her first car has been paid off, and it's now upgrade time. She is in the market for a small five door family car due to high car insurance quotations.

160

OLLIE SAVAGE

Without four of five years no claims discount, insurance is awfully expensive especially in their high car theft area. Ollie, even though he was not in the market for a car, he is taking a closer look at the second-generation Volvo XC90. It is a seven-seater with low mileage, good economy and is very spacious.

Given the many children that he has between the two women, Ollie is now buying the big Volvo for himself. He feels it is a steal at just over six grand. Deena is flabbergasted. She decides not to trade in her little Peugeot 207 but let him use it for uni while she takes the seven-seater. He can definitely benefit from the seventy-four miles per gallon on this 1.6 diesel. It is a done deal.

Nancy catches the bigger car news and surprise-surprise, she too needs an upgrade. With her own money, she trades in her e-class Mercedes for a Range Rover sport. She can afford to be flashy like that, she has earned her money the right way. Nancy discovered shares and property investments early, therefore dropping out of academia to chase real money.

She used her good credit to secure her first mortgage and a cash loan before the dawn of credit score algorithm. With the loan she bought a ton of Tesla shares and bitcoin. With the shares now skyrocketing, Nancy is old money rich.

The final year has seen Ollie at his busiest with his own dissertation and those of his clients too. Since this is where he makes most of his money, he is on a tight schedule to deliver before deadlines. With the amount of money he is projecting to make this year, that could easily be a deposit for another house.

As graduation day draws closer, Ollie really wants to impress. He has ordered his graduation gown and reserved a photographer for the special occasion. Both his women will be in attendance, alongside his sister and Caster.

As he is called up to collect his certificate, he walks with his head held high as his family and the other graduates cheer him on. They cheer on because, here is the man who has made dreams come true for a lot of students who could not have made it this far without him. Here is the man who had to invent wings to make the same journey some privileged kids had to make in a single step.

Here is the man who had beat tradition, by becoming the first from his family to not only go to university, but to graduate first class. Finally, here is a man who the devil himself had failed to cage. As he takes photos with some of the most decorated academics in the land, he smiles, because that's what the first man to climb Mount Everest did when he got to the top of that mountain.

Ollie has decided not to pursue academia any further. His big family requires him to work and provide for them. He will not be able to do that while in full time education. Some of his younger graduates have proceeded with PhD studies and are having fun, while he is now busy babysitting and writing professional CVs.

Besides his newly acquired fancy degree, Ollie has some excellent leadership skills, but he cannot get good references due to how he was leaving all those jobs. With very little experience to go by, he sends out his CVs every day and hopes for the best.

Ollie has been struggling with securing an honest job since graduating. He is as bright as they come but without the right motivation, it is sometimes hard to believe in himself. He graduated from Surrey with a first-class Honours degree in biomedical sciences.

On paper, he is the ideal candidate that any reputable employer should want to hire but then, that's just on paper. In person, he is a spiritual man, a loving husband and father to his six children. His drive comes from his spirituality and personal values.

As with most African immigrants, he wanted to graduate, get a career and buy a mortgage. As a mature graduate, there are always challenges in securing a top job. For Ollie, he has to think about the type of work, the pay rates and acceptance into the company. Most job applications do not have any responses. He moves on and keeps casting the net wider. He believes in timing. Anything can happen once the stars have aligned.

The only worry on his mind is the expiration date on his degree. Not that there is an official expiry date, but science is forever evolving. One year without a science related job following graduation, you are considered out of touch.

For a good reason, as time goes by, you start forgetting the terms and processes and before you know it, the brain gets foggy. However, Ollie enjoys reading online journals to keep up with all the latest developments in biosciences. Part reason why he does so well at interviews.

His frustration with the system is most exhibited when the job interviews yield no returns. He is very capable, but the criminal conviction he received some years ago is his biggest limiter. The desire to work hard and progress in his science field is quickly diminishing. Today's call was the last nail in the coffin.

Ollie and his wife Deena have been contemplating a relocation up north for a fresh start, since the passing of his father-in-law. Ollie's cousin Golf1 owns a highly successful garage in Manchester.

There is an MOT tester job available for him if he could just put his ego aside. An ego that Deena knows too well. She makes it about better opportunities for them as a family. The MOT job is just to pay bills until something meaningful comes up.

Deena is a critical care nurse in the NHS. She can get a job anywhere with her critical care skills. She pushes for the relocation until he gives in. It's money well spent during this transition period.

The only thing on Ollie's mind is trading in his French weather down south for some gloomy Scottish weather up north. With house hunting complete, he secures a deposit on a three-bed semi-detached house in Manchester and makes arrangements for the relocation to get underway.

The children instantly fall in love with the bigger three bed house, the front and rear gardens and bigger bathtub. Deena loves her new kitchen. It is spacious and has plenty of light and ventilation.

The lounge is way bigger and so are the bedrooms. Everything in this new house is just levels above. The best part of it all is that the purchasing price is half what they paid for the three-bed terraced house in Gillingham, Kent.

At first impressions the all-white neighbourhood is intimidating but they soon feel welcomed as the neighbours drop off welcome cards and flowers. Deena starts her new job at Wythenshawe hospital, the children start school and Ollie starts work as an MOT tester between school runs.

It works for everyone, especially Ollie. He spends time doing man's work and making a killing off MOTs. He takes one hundred quid off any potential fails. Well, he figured that was a fair price if anyone valued having a car. Given the wet weather up north, who could do without a car for a week. Just pay the man.

Golf1 is always in and out of the garage. He has his hands full with all sorts of businesses. Lately, it's been salvage cars. Something that is taking a lot of his time going to different auction centres viewing vehicles prior to online bidding. He starts to leave Ollie in charge a lot.

Ollie is learning fast. Any MOT fails are passed for a flat fee of one hundred pounds cash, of which only thirty-five pounds goes to the business. Any failure points are noted as advisories to protect the business. Unless a car is missing a headlight, a brake pedal or a steering wheel, it will pass.

Any emission fails, nonsense! Use a donor car with cleaner emissions and voila. Even though Golf1 is happy with the MOT money Ollie is raking in, he starts asking him to come along to his auctions, so he can drive the other car on the way back.

Ollie finds opportunities in everything he does, so instead of complaining about his eight hundred pounds per day job, his loyal customers will have to come back on the days he will be in the garage. In the meantime, he sticks with Golf1 and learns about this salvage business. Golf1 started off with a Golf MK1, hence his Instagram name. It was a simple car to take apart and put back together all in a day's work.

Ollie thought, why not use the same model to start his own salvage repair business, stick with one car model and master it. He decides to start off with the Vauxhall Corsas. He has given himself 3 years of repairing Corsas until he has sold a thousand MK4 Corsas. He starts off small, buying only category N cars.

What's category N cars? When cars get accident damaged, insurance companies write them off as either category N which is non-structural damage or category S, structural damage. Cat N or Cat S. Cat N is usually minor damage to the removable panels on the car like bumpers, doors, bonnets, flood damage or any minor damage such as vandalism - graffiti. Cat S is usually serious, it changes the shape of the vehicle's chassis, be it bent or broken. This includes damage to the roof, quarter panels or undercarriage.

To save money, Ollie worked on his driveway. He would strip the car off any damaged parts, buy replacement parts on eBay, spray paint them in his back garden and replace them. After a few visits to the paint shop, they knew who he was so no sweat for registration plates.

Business soon picks up and he starts to get too busy to work at Golf1's garage anymore, so, when a student mechanic comes his way looking for work experience, Ollie sends him over to Golf1 who feels it is the most admirable thing to do.

He thinks the kid is a wizard with the petrol engines. He earned his stripes at the garage that Ollie called him Wizzy, short for Wizard. Anytime he had a coughing up Corsa, Wizzy fixed it. Wizzy is all about performance. He is a real grease monkey who believes better breathing equates to better performance. Golf1 likes that about him, so much that he gives him his own set of keys, as he would sometimes work late into the night.

CHAPTER SEVENTEEN

The past six months have been an eye opener for Ollie. All he wanted was to start his own recruitment agency. His first potential contract fell through due to the unavailability of funds. The care home's owner had asked him to prove he had at least ten grand available, for paying his staff and keeping the recruitment business afloat until all invoices had been paid out.

With Ollie now leaving hustle behind him, he thought, 'who has that kind of money lain around'. He could not provide evidence of having that kind of money, unless he had good credit. The car business was not making him that much money. His pride does not allow him to beg, so even though he could easily borrow that money from Deena or Nancy, he would rather not.

Only if he had stayed in touch with Lynx, but he has too much pride. Lynx belittles people, not that he is mean, but because of the environment he was raised in. Environment is everything. It's all about the environment. The environment creates an ecosystem.

A system that enables the well informed and disables the terribly misinformed. Lynx knew too much yet Ollie knew too little of the other street. You see, when hustlers talk about the streets, there are two kinds of streets. There is the "high street" and the "common street". The high street is where all the white-collar crimes such as bitcoin fraud, dark web activity and computer hacks happen. On the common street: there are violent crimes, surrounding drugs and postcode wars.

Why hasn't he reached out you may ask? Well, their friendship only works as long as Ollie allows it to. Ollie

167

prefers a controlled environment. Like back in university for an instance, Lynx had all the money and the women. Ollie had the smarts. He did all the assignments for him, hence Lynx's first-class degree too. The assignments hustle was what led to these two meeting up.

Ollie was into that lazy white boy money, eight hundred a pop. He had earned his reputation with all the white kids. All they had to do was read it through in case any suspicions were raised. Lynx wondered how someone so smart was taking major risk for so little. Little? Eight hundred per assignment and three grand per dissertation was little? Well, given the time and energy, and compared to what Lynx was making, yeah, it was little.

Lynx had his own house and Tesla both paid for. The party life he was known for, paid for itself. Ollie believes the right crime pays. So, when Lynx got into Cunnings Banking after graduation, it was not for a career. It was for knowledge and new connections. That is high street, and Ollie liked that about him, he was decent, ambitious and loyal.

Lynx has a way with Ollie, like Caster did. He knows there are certain jobs he cannot do, so he tracks down Ollie. It takes some doing but he finally finds him. Ollie is suspicious but excited about this visit. Lynx is a phenomenal trickster. He is cutting edge, clean and way too advanced for the likes of Ollie.

When he says he has something, that's exactly what it is, he has it on lock. They spend the afternoon catching up before going into a titty bar, something Ollie has taken a liking to. Lynx whips out a small bag of snow and cuts a few lines. Ollie swiftly passes up on the offer. There are things he only associates with white boy behaviour, and this is one of them.

He has always known of Lynx's snorting since the first time he met him. He was jittery and always rubbing his nose. It never bothered Ollie or caused them any problems. Worst case is he gets insulted, but he has thick skin for it. The alternative will of course be smashing his head through a brick wall, but who needs that much attention given all the risk.

Standing by the window in his hotel room in central Manchester, the night lights aback the glass draws Lynx into a trans. He is hypnotised by the lights, running his index finger along the glass as if to feel the lights he is picking out. Ollie rings his phone to distract him from the lights. It's getting late and he hasn't said a word about the visit. Surely, he has no other business being here.

Lynx answers only to hear his own echoing voice and realises Ollie's name across his phone's screen. Ollie gathers, this man is too coked up to discuss any business. He takes him to his bedroom and tells him to rest, business will be discussed tomorrow. Lynx agrees and Ollie leaves the hotel.

Day break could not come any sooner, pregnant Deena refused to give Ollie his sleep medicine last night. It's not safe for her at this late stage of her third pregnancy. Ollie spent the night tossing and turning, primarily due to anxiety. He never sleeps well whenever he feels he has a big day ahead.

He gets ready, orders an Uber and he is on his way. He arrives back at the hotel Lynx stayed the night. They sit down and Lynx lights up a smoke. He looks smart and switched on. He barely puffs the cigarette, it's the winding patterns of the smoke that he finds therapeutic.

He asks Ollie what he knows about the dark web. "Nothing," he calmly answers. Lynx pulls out his laptop bag and fires up his MacBook Pro, to show him. He explains how it works and what opportunities it brings. He assures Ollie it's safe as long as it's in the right hands. Ollie is sold on this dark web stuff that he wants to know more.

Lynx is all ears, and his answers are satisfactory to Ollie who pulls out a small box from his man bag. Lynx's face lights up as he sees the brand name appearing on the top of the box. He opens the box and puts the watch on his arm. The bells and whistles going off in Lynx's head are so loud that Ollie almost covers his ears.

"This is madness, not you Ollie.

"No fucking way,"

He clearly associates it with the news he had followed for some years in which the people in the robbery never got caught. To confirm his suspicions, he asks Ollie how many of these he can get his hands on. Ollie tells him, "let's just say, there is more where that came from".

"You mean more like, forty of these sparkly bitches?" Ollie looks him dead in the eyes and just nods.

"Fuck me Ollie, I never saw you that way!

"What else can you do?"

"Why, you thought you white boys were the only ones running the streets, huh?"

"Come on, bring me up to speed here.

"What else, I am super anxious to know right now."

"Well, I get stuff, but right now, I own a legit business as you know.

"We haven't done anything else since then."

"We, you and someone else?"

"I have a team, they are discrete.

"Half these bitches are still out there, with my guy."

"Huh, you've got a guy Ollie.

"What does he do?"

"It's not what he does, it's what else can he do?"

"He has his own hustle out there, but when he needs bigger shit done, he comes to me."

"Oh shit, so you are his go to guy?

"Son of a bitch!

"You are so fucking dead right now.

"Why did you not tell me all this time?

"Oh, shit you didn't have my number, fuck!

"I can move all these bitches; how much do you want for them?"

"No, no, no, you see, these here are my babies.

"I won't let any of them go for less than forty."

"Forty, Ollie, are you fucking mad?

"With that shit you guys pulled off; do you know how much these are worth?

"I've got people asking for especially these.

"Guess what, eighty grand a piece!"

"No way!

"Why would they pay more, I thought they would be lower because they're hot?"

"Exactly my point.

"The right kind of hot you guys did, gives them such high value.

"Let me show you your fan page.

"Look, you guys are fucking rock stars!"

Ollie takes a minute to admire his work in the comments section, then looks at Lynx who is admiring it on his wrist too. It gives him a bit of satisfaction, just a bit.

"Ollie, look, you see this bitch right here, sold.

"I am buying this one for myself.

"Give me your details.

OLLIE SAVAGE

"I will transfer sixty grand to you, right fucking now!"

"Right now?"

"Right fucking now, give me that card!"

"Alright then, Mi Lord.

"Here, do it.

"Let me see it to believe it!"

A short moment later, Ollie receives a payment notification on his banking app, it has gone through, sixty grand. This is not business money, zero tax, sixty grand. Ollie cannot believe his luck; he had waited many years for this very moment. He looks at Lynx in pure admiration and goes for a solid handshake.

It has been the most exciting moment for the two men, that Lynx forgets to pitch his own plan to Ollie. For now, business is done. Lynx has to check in for his flight back to London in an hour. Lynx wants Ollie to get all the watches ready for pick up on the next visit. Ollie acknowledges and leaves him be.

This is really awesome business for Ollie. Little did he know, the customers were already out there waiting for these watches to appear. For every watch Lynx sells, he makes twenty grand plus for himself. There are thirty-nine more of these watches to go, and Caster has no idea what's going to hit him. There is something that caught Ollie's eye on the dark web. There was a Range Rover Sport advertised for six hundred quid. He was interested in it but he forgot to ask when Lynx had his laptop open.

It bothers him for a bit, but for now, he will settle for the sixty grand. From the hotel, Ollie passes through Golf1's garage collecting his latest acquisition, the Ford Transit Custom. Wizzy has finished the camper van conversion and upgrades

172

as per Ollie's requests. It's an ok drive for family trips but a bit underpowered for his liking.

As he pulls onto his drive, he knows there is no 'backsliding' from here. It is either go hard or go home, and home in particular is not a choice for him. He locks the van and gets into the castle that is his home. He is greeted by the kids who innocently run into him and hangs on to each leg, as they express their longing for him. His wife can only smile as he rolls on to the floor with them while shouting for help to mama, as if they are hurting him.

This gentle giant side of him is reserved only for his women and children. He hugs and kisses Deena and sneaks in some quick reading time with the children before she orders for the table to be cleared, ready for dinner. Here, in the confines of his castle, he is just a pile of mush.

He opens his MacBook Air and goes through his emails. Unfortunately, the other care home owner he has been banking on for his recruitment business has passed the contract on to someone else. In the email he wrote that he could not associate his business with someone with a criminal conviction. It simply goes against his company's values.

That's all the extra motivation Ollie needed. He thinks to himself, from here on, fuck all these people telling me I am not good enough! From here on, he does it his way. The sixty grand in his account is all the head start he ever needed, now it's a level playing field.

CHAPTER EIGHTEEN

With the new money he got from the watch, he knows he has his foot in the door. He registered his business, opened a business bank account and got into an auto body repair business. The name Ollie Savage was a mistake by the kid he paid to do the shop's graphics, who misspelled Ollie's Salvage and it quickly caught on as Ollie Savage.

Now banks were calling, offering him overdrafts. Loan companies he had never heard of were now calling him, offering loans and credit cards. What would he do, given all that financial attention? He consulted Lynx, his trusted advisor.

Ollie learnt how to manage money from Lynx, who was taught about money at home by both his parents who are extremely wealthy. He taught Ollie that, to be financially independent, he needs to invest more than he spends. If he cannot buy any luxury item ten times over, then he has no business buying it. He advised him two things, that is:

To invest ninety percent of every grand he makes.
To never work for money payments, but only to learn a trade.

Ollie started accepting all those overdrafts, loans, and credit cards only to invest the money into his own business. He hired a qualified auto body technician and some apprentices through the government scheme. He got paid by the government to get them trained. He would buy salvage cars, repair them then sell them on.

Once he made profits from the cars, he would pay the loans back early, to avoid high interest rates. Every 'commoner' in the UK knows Barclays bank, Halifax, NatWest and so on. Ollie started receiving calls from private banks that are off the grid. How did they find him, they would

174

simply follow the money. This was now unfamiliar territory, and as such, he needed some of Lynx's counsel.

With the autobody business going so well, it was only a matter of time before he tried his hand at car wrapping. There was only one place doing real nice car wraps but Golf1 had the link. Ollie arranged for a business lunch as they have always done but this time, Ollie only needs information. After their lunch, Golf1 took Ollie to 'The Indians', Indie's crew.

Meeting Indie was a game changer. Indie and his team can wrap up real nice, and quick. His test Corsa is done in under eight minutes. It looks slick, he wants to go further and turn it into a sleeper. Indie likes his vibe; he gives him his phone number so they can do more business in the future. Ollie has enough work for him, so it makes business sense for both parties.

As though by fate, Caster contacts Ollie first, through social media. Ollie reads the message, 'SOS' and sees the made-up name, he knows straight away who this is. They exchange burners and Caster makes the call straight away. He is desperate and pushy; Ollie knows he wants something, or something done.

"SOS, why don't that surprise me?"

"I am well thanks, how have you been?"

"Well, you know me, just out here in the land of the white man".

"Why Manchester though?"

"And how come you never told me you were moving?"

"I thought we're family?"

"Well, it was last minute.

"I had to get my family out of there.

"It was getting hot with the law and everything."

"Why, what happened?
"My father in-law's body was pulled out of River Medway man."
"Shit, what happened?"
"I had hit him, so he tried putting a hit on me."
"Shit, Ollie! How did you find out about the hit?"
"He had tried using my guys."
"Shit, so they 'offed' him?"
"Ay man, I didn't kill him.
"He got a taste of his own shit. "Ay, why did you really call man, got something for me?"
"You're a crazy ma' fucker, Ollie! "Yeah, I need some help, they are giving my Bro fifteen years. "I have run out of money for lawyers man, cut me some cards."
"Wait, you mean Goldie, what for, what has he done now?"
"V.A.T refunds, States side.
"It's all over Facebook, these fucking lawyers man!
"I need money quickly or I sell my assets. "I need like, thirty to forty grand!".
"Shit, I'm sorry Bro. "How is Nancy dealing with it?"
"She is tough, she'll be fine."
"Oh good.
"Yeah, I can definitely help man.
"He is my crazy Bro too man.
"Let me hit you up in a minute, I might have something for you real soon, hold tight."
"Ok, one."

Despite starting off on the wrong foot, Goldie is like a brother to Ollie too, so this really fucks with his day. Goldie is the original gangster. He made these boys the men they are today. He was out there driving Type S Jaguars, Range Rovers and drop top Bimmers way back when all Zambanians were just getting papers and going into nursing.

Ollie doesn't sit on it too long; he calls Caster back on the same burner.

"Cas, you may speak!"

"Listen to yourself, still on that 'You may speak' bullshit.

"You aren't fooling me!"

"Seriously, speak.

"What have you got for me?"

"You still got them hot bitches?"

"All twenty, why?"

"Word?"

"Word, no bullshit."

"Good, I got a link.

"He wants all in, but only at one point five a piece."

"Shit, he is mad.

"What else?"

"Look man, this is the help.

"That shit is hot, and not one person in their right mind, wants to touch that.

"Call me back!"

Ollie knows it's not even considerable, given that it's Audemars. Hold that thought, Caster is calling him.

"Ollie, you may speak!"

"Yoh, let me hold that forty grand, and your guy can have all twenty."

"My man!

"Will hit you back."

"Not long, I ain't got no time!"

"One."

Ollie ends the call on 'one love'. This transaction once more confirms Ollie's belief that selling your soul really depends on the right offer. Caster just made the forty grand he needs to free his brother. Ollie has helped an old friend free his brother while fairly acquiring the rest of them bitches, at two grand a piece.

As per routine, Ollie always gives his wife some really good thrusting after a good day's work. Intimacy is no longer a common occurrence these days. It is consensual but, without full engagement. Deena is still bitter as she tries to re-establish feelings for him following his most recent infidelity with her younger sister, Linda.

With Nancy still down south and Linda taking her place with childcare, Ollie had struggled fighting off the temptation that spans back a few years. Linda is just too hot for Ollie. She is taller, more beautiful and an extrovert. Deena had always seen the threat in her; hence she had banned her from her house after catching her on his lap kissing him, back in Godalming.

How did it go down this time round? You and your inquisitive little mind! I wasn't supposed to tell this part but, I respect your appreciation for gossip. Anyway, I am glad you asked, let's run it back. So, Deena asks Linda to temporarily move in and help out with the kids for a while, until she secures a reliable babysitter. It is an old romance between Ollie and Linda since she came back.

While Deena is at work, Linda is sending Ollie some raunchy pictures and videos, explicitly showing off her beautifully shaved pussy. I know, right! So, listen. Ollie leaves his men working and tells them he is going home for brunch. With the kids at nursery, Ollie steps into the house only to be met at the door by Linda, who is naked. He takes his overalls off and picks her up, carrying her up the flight of stairs and into the shower. She rests her back on the wall, while wrapping her legs around him. Horny bitch!

"Why are you being rough with me? I thought you'd take me to the bedroom and fuck me on your wife's bed," she asks him.

"What makes you think am going to fuck you? Remember we only tease but don't fuck."

"Really, why did you come running after I sent you pics of my shave?"

"I was coming home for brunch anyway."

"So why carry me into the shower, am I the brunch you came for?"

"No, just satisfying whatever this thing in your head is."

"Mmm, why is your dick all drippy then, it's making me even wetter," she said, grabbing it and positioning its head onto her wet pussy.

He lets her rest on it, while kissing her. This time, she is a bit more accommodating. He lightly tip-teases her, making her pussy relax a bit more. She starts whining on his tip while kissing him, then she finally howls as he suddenly pierces her, shuttering her hymen. She bleeds on him quite a bit, that some blood runs down his leg.

"Are you ok, I have never seen so much virgin blood?"

"Aww, it fucking hurts. Gently please," she holds on to him as he slowly burrows deeper into her. He keeps to a steady pace as she continues lubricating on him. The bleeding soon stops, and he puts her down, drenching in sweat. He turns her over, dips lower to her height, before penetrating her from behind, doggy style.

Surely but gently, he starts picking up momentum as she finds the doggy deeply pleasurable. She pleads with him to slow down whenever she can't take the ramming and encourages him to ram into her again when she needs it deeper.

Figuring she won't come with the traditional deep thrusting, he shallow tips her concentrating on her engorged g-spot until she starts squirting. He pulls out as she rips and shoves it back in once it's all out. He finally grabs her by her wide hips and jackhammers the shit out of her, releasing his load inside her.

"OMG, are you trying to get me pregnant on the first day?"

"Nah, you won't get pregnant, I know your cycle."

"Really, stalker alert," she said, switching on the shower.

"My lower abdomen hurts so bad. It felt like someone was stabbing me through my vajay-jay."

"Wait until tomorrow, you won't be able to laugh, cough or sneeze."

"I don't care, I'm just glad we've done it. At least now I know everything works as it should."

"My goodness, you have the sweetest pussy in the world. Woo!"

"Now I know you're just saying that to make me feel good about myself."

"Nah, Linda listen, you have one sweet pussy. Not that I must compare but, you are special. And that squirting, bananas."

"Yeah, is that why you were groaning that loud?"

"No, I did not!"

"Yes, you did. You should see your sex faces; you look ugly as fuck."

"Now that's mean, take it back."

"I will not, but I can kiss you. You have the most amazing lips. Come here."

They passionately kiss and caress under the steamy shower until Ollie calls time and dashes back to work. "It's finally

180

done," he tells himself, still trying to wrap his head around it. The replays in his mind turn him on again that he turns back around and flows it, as he goes back to the house for seconds.

He finds her doing her makeup in front of the bathroom mirror and carries her into his bedroom and throws her onto the bed. "What are you doing, I just showered."
"Look, you turn me on so much, I was on my way to work when my dick just screamed your name. I had to come back, give me that sweet pussy again," he said, undressing her.
Now knowing she too, like her sister, is a squirter, he reaches into the bed storage and grabs a fresh towel which he places under her buttocks.

He sucks her nipples and kisses and caresses her fast. She tells him to slow down but he goes in rough and hard. He dicks her out. She pleads with him to be gentle, but it falls on deaf ears. He fucks her deeper and deeper until he feels her pubic bone digging into his. He keeps it deep, buried inside her hot and wet pussy.

Even he knows he has never fucked anyone like this before, which makes her special. She digs her nails deep into him in response to his thrusts as she climaxes, her pussy walls tighten and squeezes his dick until a warm, milky-cream gushes out of her pussy. She growls as he pounds her even harder and deeper as he gets his second nut. He slumps into her, resting his sweaty body over her.
"I cannot breathe, get off me."
"Sorry babe, let me just catch my breath."
"Shit, so all that time I was hearing her moan like that, you were actually laying some serious pipe?"
"You never heard anything; she is not as loud as you."
"She definitely is louder than me. "OMG, you finally fucked me, properly. "You can fuck, I give you that. "You had left

me wondering if that was it, the mighty-mighty work of Ollie, the savage."

"Oh, I was being gentle because it was your first time. I did not want to give you my best shot just yet."

"I definitely don't mind if this was your best shot. You made me cum so hard, I thought my heart was gonna stop. "How many 'dicker' awards have you got?"

"Well, only three for now. One from Deena, one from Nancy and one from you I guess."

Oh, no. Uh-uh! You can fool those two bitches into fighting over your dick but not me, oh no!"

"What, so you just wanted me to break you and that's it?"

"Yeah, fool! "There is no cuddling up afterwards. "No catchy feelies here! "It's straight up business, mmm, mmm! I don't play that shit."

"Really? You are one stone cold woman!"

"You can go back to work now, bye. "Dismissed!"

Ollie goes back into the shower and Linda follows him. She gets in and washes him with a soapy sponge spinning him around, it's a good wash. She squirts some soap into her hand and washes off his dick, only to find it erecting again. She laughs as she cannot believe his stamina.

This is what her sister meant when she complained about his never-ending appetite. She sucks him off until he gets real hard, then she bends over and gives him another doggy. He pounds her without holding back as she lets him rip. The sweetness of her fresh and tight pussy makes him cum even quicker this time round. She does not complain of getting cut off as she had done this for him. They shower and he finally goes back to work.

Ollie and Nancy only talk on the phone these days. Ollie has missed her and the kids so much but his terms with Deena don't allow him to just up and leave. With that in mind, he takes his frustration out on Linda, who is only happy to continue laying with him, but is not catching feelings for him. Either that or she just knows how to hide them better.

Being the extrovert and adventurous type, she has persuaded Ollie to finally try anal sex with her. They have a go at it lying down and standing up until Ollie's dick finally collapses on him. It's just not happening, every time he tries, no amount of lube works as his dick just stalls on him. They stick to what they know, and Ollie keeps delivering every time, but Linda won't catch or display any feelings. It breaks his heart, but he remains optimistic.

It doesn't take long before Deena starts having her suspicions about Ollie and Linda again. This time Deena has solid evidence. Confronted with Linda's knickers that she had left in their bed, Ollie knew better than lying to her or denying it. Since owning up to sleeping with his sister, Deena has once kicked her out of their house.

It has taken a minute to heal this time round. It only takes longer to heal with each strike. He does not have the luxury of time to wait for her to come around as he believes she is running away from the cure each time she says no to intimacy.

This time she softly cries as he hammers away. She can't help but wonder if this is exactly what he did to her sister. He pulls out and unloads onto her breasts and belly. He leans over her and rubs his ejaculate all over her protruding baby belly, breasts, neck and face. "I declare this body be cleansed from all manners of negative energy," he murmurs. She does not stop him as she continues to whimper. He kisses her on the sodden forehead and slumps to his side of the bed for a deep coma like sleep. She quietly sneaks out of bed to wash off his unpleasant rub and get some much-needed quality time with her buzzing new friend, 'Tracy's Dog'. Oh, you are such a dafty, that's that famous vibrator from Amazon.

With all the noise going on around Ollie, Lynx has been quiet since their last conversation. Ollie tolerates his disappearing acts for a reason. Last time he was up north, he made Ollie too much money, no wonder he is excited about his return. Today's scheduled meeting is of mighty importance.

He is supposed to be at Ollie Savage by now. Ollie is all about principle, if you say one o'clock and you realise, you're running late then call him. When that does not happen, he starts playing the different worst-case scenarios in his head and that drains him.

The young lady collecting her mended Renault Clio is driving him mad, she is too flirtatious and claims she does not have enough money to pay the remainder on her repairs. Ollie pulls the shutters down; in case she tries driving off without full payment.

She has picked the wrong day to be childish; Ollie invites her into the office upstairs and closes the door behind him. She laughs off at the angry face he puts on, but he does not see the joke. He takes the belt off his pants and strikes the desk with it.

"Listen woman, I don't have enough money too, but I still pay my rates here. "Don't let this good day end with your kidnap. "Do you understand me?"

"Oh, please Mr Mechanic, you are scaring me.

"I must warn you; I am very fragile," as she turns and bends over the office desk.

"Please dear sir, mind the white skin, it bruises," she said, seeing Ollie raise his belt.

"Well, how did you allow it to escalate this far, pay the difference" as he strikes her once across her firm buttocks.

"Oh, I think that's enough punishment. "Sir please, let me help calm you down, please sit right here," she ties her hair back.

"How will that get me my money?"

With one arm wrapping around his neck, she kisses him ever so gracefully and slides her warm hand down the front inside of his pants, awakening his monster cock.

Noticing the punishment is quicky turning into role play, he plays along, "Do not be such a nuisance woman, pay me my goddamn money."

"Sir, what are you packing in here?" she mumbles as she wrestles with his anaconda, uncoiling it from its layer and guides it into her seemingly tiny mouth.

She teases his tip back and forth sucking and slurping then tucks it all the way to the back of her throat. He groans in the intensity of the propulsions from her throat. She chokes, gags and spits on his tip as she gives him head like no other, thereby exposing his weakness.

A few dips to the back of her throat and he intensely nuts in her mouth. She happily receives all of him, tongue clicking and slurping until she has caught every last drop of his cum. "Bad bitch!" he said, looking at her beautiful face.

"Thank you sir, pleasure doing business with you."

"You are welcome!".

Ollie's heart is racing. He smiles as she swings her hips side to side leaving his office. He zips up and reaches for the remote. The shutters are rolled up remotely as he shouts, "keys are in the ignition."

185

A few moments later, his phone rings and Ollie answers.

"Mi Lord, is that you?"

"Is it safe to come in now?"

"Of course, Mi Lord, please do come in!"

Lynx pulls up in his new Model X and looks around at what Ollie has built.

"Money well spent; I say!"

"Thank you, Lord Lynx."

"You need to stop with that Mi Lord shit.

"It ain't funny with all that's going on out there, seriously!"

"Fuck that, all lives matter Mi Lord, all lives matter!"

"Oh, someone was enjoying some white pussy!"

"Fuck off man, you jealous I overstretched your sister's pink pussy."

"Your sister has got pink pussy too if you look inside next time!"

"Ew, enough with the sister jokes man, why are you here?"

"Money man, I've brought you a ton of money.

"How much money do you have right now Ollie?

"To make it fair, sum up all your assets too?

"How much would you say you are worth?"

"Ma' fucker, the business money belongs to my wife and the crown.

"So that leaves me with the sixty grand you gave me last time."

"Shit, Ollie, then you might be happy to learn that I, Lord Lynx, do hereby solemnly declare you a millionaire, as of today.

"That is, if you have all my shit ready."

"A millionaire?

"Alright then Mi Lord, this way please.

"Accompany me to the office."

"You know what Ollie, you would have made an excellent actor.

"Have you ever considered it?"

"What, are you forgetting something?

"I am black, man. Original black.

"Ain't nobody wanting to see my Kunta Kinte ass on tv, shit."

"You see, barrier."

"Where?"

"In your head, you don't give yourself enough credit Ollie.

"You lack self-belief.

"What a fucking pity!"

"Nah, pity ain't got nothing to do with it.

"I lack funding, Mi Lord.

"It's only educated fools like you, that see all that shit myself or the people around me fail to see."

"Now that is something we can both agree on.

"Anyway, you won't believe this?"

"What?"

"It took some doing, but I have managed to sort you out with the right bank account.

"To top that, your main branch is in Chekwa, Zambani, where your wealth is protected.

"Now tell me, who loves yah?"

"What, how does that even work?"

"I was right here the whole time?"

"Listen, there goes that negativity.

"What's my name, what do I do?"

"Pardon me, Mi Lord.

"Good intentions intended."

"Right, it's all legit.

"They have approved your national identity card, they have confirmed all your UK identities i.e. driver's licence and business bank statements."

"Did you tweak the statements?"

"Standard procedure, my son.

"Now, like me, you too can move your money around the world as you wish."

"Here, your login details.

"Login and change your passwords and I will show you what else."

Ollie logs into his new account, looks at the balance and starts to tremble. He is shocked to see the long numbers that are his account's balance. Lynx had deposited three million, one hundred and twenty thousand pounds. As he tries to absorb it all in, he wonders when this figure will just vanish.

He logs out then back in again, but his balance has not changed. He takes a deep breath and brings his hands to prayer position.

"Boy, what have you done, is this a prank?"

"Prank, nah. Ollie look, I am wealthy and so are my parents, but you already knew that.

"Have you heard of bitcoin?"

"Come on, you are doing it again, belittling me.

"Of course, I know about crypto, get to the fucking point!"

"Good, we are on the same page.

"So, those eighty grand watches, I auctioned a few of them for feels.

"Auction ends in approximately... four hours.

"Look, people are going crazy over them on the dark web.

"You see, here look, this is my Coinbase wallet. "This is what I also transferred to your Coinbase wallet earlier.

"What, I have eighty bitcoins in my wallet right now, how much is that?"

"Just multiply it by today's rate of twelve thousand.

"Ollie focus! Look, I have already made three point five million, pound sterling, worth of bitcoin from a few of those bitches.

"People can't wait for the auction to end; they are already buying outright Ollie!"

"Shit, how much stock should we have?"

"Nah Ollie, the fewer the better.

"These will do for now.

"Once the ratings come in, no one can touch us.

"Next time, we will do something else, Jacob & Co type shit.

"Watch this space!"

"Wait, next time?"

"Yeah, fucking next time Ollie, we are officially in business now my son.

"No more small money, just keep this warehouse open.

"Depending on how the auction finishes, I will deposit more bitcoin into your wallet later. "I fucking live for this bitcoin shit!"

This fool is terribly misinformed in thinking Ollie would pull something like that ever again. Ollie goes silent. The new money, the bitcoin and the "next time" statement is worrisome. It's all happening way too fast. He needs to let it all sink in. He walks out into the car park to get some air, leaving Lynx to his computer components upstairs.

He thinks about how much time and effort, the ridiculous number of sleepless nights and the constant shagging that's needed to keep his sanity while planning jobs of a reasonable size. Now that he has tasted the fruits of hard work, Ollie is very tempted by the opportunity to take on an even bigger job with higher rewards. What could Lynx have that might get him to commit to another job, he wonders.

He decides to go and ask for himself while Lynx is still here. He can't stand his disappearing acts. Most of the time, he is left wondering whether he would ever come back again. What he does not know is, Lynx knows too well Ollie can deliver, so he never approaches him without something solid, because once Ollie commits, there is no going back.

"So, Lynx, on this dark web of yours, I saw some nice flashy cars on there: Range Rover Sports, Jaguars, Lamborghinis and stuff.

"What's going on with those?"

"Oh, those, it's people selling them, but they are hot. "It's usually all these kids selling their parents' cars without their knowledge, and then reporting them stolen.

"Remember they are hot, you don't need anything like that in your life right now, you're a millionaire now."

"Listen, say I bought one of them, do I get it delivered?"

"Look Ollie, like I said to you, you're a millionaire now, you don't need anything like that in your life, ever."

"I know that, and thanks for looking out for me, but I'm not asking for myself.

"I know someone, who can benefit from something like that, someone who's in that line of business."

"Tell me and I might just help you."

"Look, there's this guy in London that I used to work with, he's going through a rough moment right now, and could really do with some extra money."

"Look, Ollie, you can't just tell me some basic lie and expect me to believe you.

"I want details, how do you know this guy?"

"He is my brother, he needs work."

"Nah Ollie, we can't just bring in people like that.

"Some of these people are just not smart enough, we need to work with only smart people."

"I know that, but this guy, that is his business.

"He's been shipping these cars back home for years now.

"He has his link; he knows how to get around it."

"Ok then, as long as it won't burn you, because I have plans for you."

"About that, give me an idea of what we are talking about here.

"What sort of gear would I need, I need time to prepare you know that, right?"

"This won't be no smash and grab; this will be a really big job.

"You might need to get a car ready, a proper getaway car though."

"I'm in.

"When is it for, what's your time frame?

"I need time to prepare Lynx."

"Get a car ready, call me and then I'll take it from there."

"Nah, you know I don't work like that.

"I do all the planning."

"Not this job, it's not that type.

"I will give you more information once you are ready."

"Lynx, when it comes to getting away, driving getaway, remember, I'm your guy. "So, let me plan this thing properly please."

"Get the car ready and let me know.

"Make sure it's a big, fast car, maybe a BMW estate.

"We will need tons of space."

At Ollie Savage, Ollie is getting his hands dirty helping out his boys get the cars ready for Friday collections. Everybody has their role, from dents pulling and sanding, filling and sanding, base quoting and sanding. Once the cars are finally sprayed with a clear coat, they are left in the shop to dry overnight. Tomorrow morning, they start polishing and collections should start by lunch time.

Ollie is more dedicated to his business now than ever. Every morning, he wakes up to a five o'clock alarm and takes a thirty-minute cold shower. He brushes his teeth, gets dressed and says his morning prayers at exactly six o'clock.

The programmed coffee dispenser gets started and brews him a strong-fresh mug of ground coffee, which he takes straight, no additives. He goes into his safe and grabs some change for the day. He puts on his steel toe cap boots, grabs his hat and keys, then hopes into the car and is off to work.

At work he spends the entire day making sure there are no shenanigans taking place with his money or compromise in the quality of his work. Every person has their own role to play. That way, if anything goes wrong, he knows exactly whose balls to crush.

He runs this auto body as he ran his hustle back in the day, with precision. When all the targets have been met, people can now go home. The profits from Ollie Savage are enabling him to acquire properties, both commercial and residential. He is ok with the slow processes associated with making legit money but, it's money that has a good paper trail.

CHAPTER NINETEEN

Lynx is in town today. Since the last time they met, he had been quiet, one of his character traits Ollie has grown to love. He appears and disappears when needed. That way, there is barely enough time to clash heads with Ollie who can be a hot head sometimes.

With the workers on target and having finished early, it has created ample time for Ollie and Lynx to discuss business.

"Ollie, do you know my last name?"

"Buchanan, is it not?"

"Not quite.

"Buchanan is my middle name.

"My last name is Rhodes, ringing any bells?"

"Oh yeah, it does have a ring to it.

"Southern Africa Rhodes, is that the one?"

"Smart man, you see, he was my great grand-father. "He and his team went on an expedition, to explore the so-called dark continent for territory and precious minerals. "He wound up settling in one of your regions, naming it after himself..."

"Where are you going with this Lynx, do I die in the end?"

"Just listen, alright! "He did very well exporting ivory, gold, diamonds and other precious collectibles. "He was my blood relative, but he went too far. "Long story short, we have our name to protect. "Our name is one of the biggest names out there. "It means a lot to a lot of proud people but, here is the catch, it means more on the dark web. "If you can get your hands on some of these collectibles we have, you are set for life. "The best part is, you are entitled to this wealth Ollie, it's from your region, Southern Africa. That's why I want you in on it."

"Wait a minute, so don't people of your kind go to Oxford and that? "How did you end up at Surrey, with the likes of me?"

"Don't believe the hype, besides, I never was one for following the rules anyway. "Look at me, I am here in this fucking cold warehouse. I told you from day one, I am a commoner."

"Those types of people Lynx, they guard shit.

"It sounds to me like, the type of treasure you are talking about, needs guarding.

"Wouldn't you agree, or did you forget to mention that part, security?"

"I was getting to that.

"There are cameras that are monitored by some private security firm, but I can easily bypass them.

"And, we are also allocated two armed police guards, real police officers, day and night."

"Jail time, nice!

"Bye-bye Lynx!"

"Listen, these officers do not have back up.

"The next police unit is miles out."

"You do not touch the police, period!"

"Look, if no one gets hurt, we are good.

"Just do not hurt nobody, yeah?"

"They are armed police officers, they kill black people, Lynx!"

"Ollie, I have seen these guys work.

"They have been guarding us their whole working lives.

"Nothing happens there, nothing has ever happened. "Well, besides me hacking them every now and then."

"Oh, my goodness, you're getting better each time I let you speak.

"Get out, Lynx!

"Leave my office now, please!"

Lynx walks down the stairs hoping Ollie calls him back. Ollie lets him leave the garage and goes back into his office to call him. He eagerly answers the phone after one ring.

"That was quite intense.

"Gosh Ollie, I hate you!"

"Get your narrow ass back in here before I change my mind," he hangs up the phone. Ollie wanted to establish control. He needed to remind Lynx who is in control here. If he can control the way Lynx thinks, he can control the outcome. This is Ollie's own algorithm with people.

"My question to you Lord Lynx is, what's in it for you?

"Surely you cannot just hand it to me on a silver platter.

"What do you want out of all this?"

"I expected that one.

"Obviously, I get more out of these collectibles now."

"Elaborate."

"If the goods are sold hot now, I make more money than I will when I finally get in line to inherit them.

"Our target market is unique, it's all about power to them.

"They feel powerful when there is some type of ingenious notoriety behind the items they acquire."

"Keep talking."

"That's why cars, guns and drugs sell cheap, that's old. "There is no plot behind that staff, only blood in and blood out. "These guys, they respect smarts over brutality. "It's like a 'go fund me' for smart criminals. "People like us. "You and me Ollie!"

"So, you're my sidekick now, huh? "What if your people chose not to report it. "What if they chose to protect their name over humiliation, and we are stuck with unsellable shit?"

"They will have to, for insurance. Otherwise, we will figure out how to force their hand, but just remember, you get the lion's share, Ollie. "You get some sort of revenge for your people and country. "You will be an unsung hero when the dust settles. "Only you will know what you did for your country. "You will humiliate the Rhodes."

"Mmm, I am not sold on this, Lynx. "There is no *je ne sais quoi*, no real street cred in this ingenious notoriety of yours."

"Fuck street cred, Ollie! "You are above that now. "Millionaires do not associate with street cred.

"They care about legacy, real world legacy.

"What did street cred get you when you were stuck with them watches?

"Think millions Ollie, millions yeah?"

"So, I get to do this for my people's revenge, huh?"

"Yeah, something like this has never been done to people of power Ollie.

"My loyalty is to you and me. "Our team, period!"

"You are a cold ma' fucker, Lord Lynx.

"Your great granddaddy must be very proud."

"Not as proud as yours mate.

"You'd have finally brought pride to your ancestors."

"Ok, Mi Lord. Give me every little detail so I can work my magic.

"I mean everything!"

When it was finally time to get a getaway car, Ollie went about it the usual way, the better have and not need way. Ollie needed the help of one resourceful young man to start working on his next project car. To his surprise, when he asked to borrow Wizzy, the enthusiastic apprentice working for his cousin Golf1, he gladly released him from his contract due to the tight money coming his way.

Now working around the clock at Ollie Savage, Wizzy is stripping down Ollie's family camper van and rebuilding it from scratch.

"Hey, Wizzy, how is it coming along?"

"Hey Boss, I'm still tearing it apart."

"I thought I said, make it better not worse, how is tearing it apart reaching our goal?"

"Chill boss, sometimes the surgeon has to cut up a patient to make them better."

"Yeah, where did you learn that?"

"My dad, he is a tree surgeon, a good one too."

Ollie is caught off guard and rips a hearty laugh, "So you tell girls your father is a surgeon yeah, smart kid" he continues laughing.

"I have always loved these Transit Customs, they are badass," he tells Ollie.

"I am installing the 2000 horse engine from that racing boat you want to scrap."

"Is that still any good?"

"It runs, but I will strip it, clean and make it brand new to make sure it performs."

"Boat engine, really, with all these new engines sitting around here?"

"Boat engines barely do any serious mileage; it's still good.

"Besides, the wiring is easier."

"Your head, kid."

"Trust me Ollie, everyone has access to those car engines.

"That one there, only you will have it.

"It's going to be a bit loud, but the power, woo!

"This thing will easily do two eighty to three twenty miles per hour, when I'm through with it."

"What else do you need?"

"I have ordered all the parts I need and we are still within our budget.

"It's literally going to be a racing bus on steroids, Ollie."

"Well, my wife will also be driving it, just make sure she won't crash and burn in that thing."

Nancy and her football team have visited. They are spending two weeks in Ollie's newly acquired 'B&B' while having a feel of the city. London is too far for Ollie to visit and has been straining their relationship. Ollie wants Nancy close by so he can see her and the kids every day. He is hoping she likes the place he has bought for her but he is not be telling her just yet.

"This is an excellent location I must say. I like the location and the privacy."

"Thanks mama."

"Five bed, you'll definitely make so much money once this place is in full swing. That's if they can find it in these woods."

"Well, I leant from the best. "I am not worried about the location, that's why there is navigation."

"Point. I like the décor, it's traditional but elegant."

"I stole it from your first one."

"I can see that.

"What was wrong with the original glass, single glazed?"

"Yeah, it's way colder up here.

"Even during this summer, our temperatures are still lower."

"I can tell, but we will adapt, no?"

Nancy seems to like where Ollie is going. She sees a lot of potential in him, but most importantly, he is keeping his promise to her. Even though he has other commitments with Deena and the autobody business, she does feel included. This level headedness is what made her fall in love with him to start with. She knows his heart. So, when she said, "we will adapt," it's a signal to him that we are in this together.

This is a good day, not just for them both, but the 'twinsies' too who seem to love this house just as much. They cannot conceal their excitement that they wake the sleeping baby up. Ollie goes over and picks her up from the Moses basket and comforts her with kisses. Given that this fifth child is the first of Nancy's singleton after the two sets of twins - *twinsies*, this one is the special one to him.

"Sorry mama, we woke you up so you can see your new home. "Look, you are going to be living here in Manchester with me, ok. "Welcome home mama."

"Really, you bought this for us? "Oh my God, I love you so much," screams Nancy hugging him. "Oh, I love it baba. This is such a perfect home for us. I love it, love it, love it," she says looking around and running into the garden to tell the twinsies.

His daughter seems to understand what he has just told her. She has grown on him so much. His love for her is clearly displayed by the way he canoodles her. If it were not for Nancy who pleads with him to put her down, he would spoil her rotten, but she wants her to learn to be independent fast. This allows her to get housework done.

Ollie has spent some much-needed time with Nancy and the children, breaking them in and helping them feel at home here. Nancy loves her new home so much; she cannot wait for the relocation to get underway. She has movers on standby for when she is ready.

Caster, who arrived by train to collect them, has offered to help once they are back in London. This is what he wanted for them for quite some time now. He assures Ollie that he will push for the move from his end, so she does not sit on it. He is pleased to learn that Ollie is doing so well up north and is surely tempted to follow suit and register a legitimate business.

"I love it here Bro.

"It's quiet.

"Can you help me set up shop here man?"

"Anytime, Bro. How did it go with Goldie?"

"Oh, he got bail, and fled back home. Thanks for the link man. It helped."

"No problem man. Anytime you're ready let me help you set up. On the house.

"You cannot hustle the streets forever man.

"It's a young man's game, we have kids and women to look after now."

"I know man, I know.

"How do you do it, how do you make it work man?

"How do you control your women?"

"That's the problem right there.

"No woman wants to be controlled, man.

"Just make them feel loved, appreciated and valued.

"Let a woman know she means the world to you, and she will stand by you to the death man.

"You can't act that shit; it has to come from your heart man.

"That's it."

"Listen to you Ollie, sounding all philosophical and shit.

"Set me up soon," said Caster, as he reaches to shake Ollie's hand before setting off for London. As Caster drives off Nancy's latest XC90 so harshly, Ollie chuckles knowing it's just for show. The kids have changed their uncle's driving since the days of his CLS500.

Following some serious work around the clock, Wizzy has finally finished Ollie's getaway vehicle, disguised as a family camper van. It looks subtle-ish and bears the sticker "Hit what you can see" on its rear glass. Ollie is impressed by the modifications he has made. The driving is smoother than he anticipated but the frightening power is a concern for his wife.

Once the turbo kicks in, it glues you to your seat, but the body is well balanced. It holds traction so well that there is no body roll. The adaptive air suspension has made it smooth like butter. He was worried the engine's power would overwhelm the other systems sending the whole thing spinning out of control. It is a well-deserved earning and a very good reputation Wizzy has built with Ollie.

The plan is complete, and Ollie has his gadgetry and specialized men on standby. For all their help with the job, they will each receive a cash lump sum after the job is completed. It is paramount for them as it is for Ollie, that the job is completed successfully, or they risk it all for nothing. Lynx gave Ollie a key piece of information.

The armed police officers guarding his family fortress had become too comfortable. The Rhodes had requested that only a team of four officers work for them to avoid disruption with reorienting new officers each time. There were two armed police officers per shift, day and night.

They had probably never pulled their guns out except in training exercises since leaving their police academies.

They were so out of touch with the realities of daylight robberies that when they were finally faced with true criminals with bigger guns aimed at them, they simply froze.

Ollie and his men secured their guns and handcuffed them before loading them into the van. Lynx, who had hacked into the security systems and jammed their communications, led the way into the property followed by Ollie and his team. They began ransacking the property for some special collectibles.

However tempting elephant tasks, among other larger items were to take, they were just too bulky for Ollie's bother. They only took the smaller items of higher value. Prior to the robbery, Lynx had made a list of the most valuable items and they stuck with it. They loaded up and narrowly made a getaway just before the police units could surround them, getting a head start.

Ollie's getaway driver, an ex-military Navman calmly navigated the getaway route choices Ollie had pre-approved. Zones was a British army trained Navman who had retired after he had served in Iraq and Afghanistan. His Navman training gave him knowledge of the off-grid routes that are not accessible to the common British citizen. The getaway routes were truly Zones' specialty and more suited to their airless tyres and the adaptive air suspension Wizzy had fitted to the van.

The police cars simply failed to handle the terrain and the two and half thousand horses the van was throwing. The minor problem was the police chopper that stayed above them for a while. Once they hit a stretch, the helicopter quickly reached its maximum speed limit and fizzled into the horizon. They are just not designed for high-speed chases of that magnitude.

Indie and his crew had done a great job of carefully concealing police themed stickers under a couple of wrapping films. The first wrapping film was removed as soon as they left the Rhodes residence. Hence the vehicle colour change from blue to black threw off some of the police cars. The black film was removed once they had lost the police cars and the chopper once they went off grid.

After they removed the black wrapping film from the van, they became the law and joined the motorway disguised as the police with a matching police registration plate. Last stop was the services where the helpers were paid off and left to arrange their individual transport home. That way, there was no repeat of the past.

The paint shop guys had done a lot of business with Ollie for too long, they did not sweat him for registration plates. He had over ten spare sets of plates printed off for the Rhodes job, when he only needed a few. The registration plates were changed at motorway services and some along the way to and from the job as Ollie instructed.

Before printing, all the plates were confirmed live by HPI checks. Their respective vehicles were taxed, insured and MOTd. This was to avoid being picked up by the ANPR system on most traffic police vehicles and road cameras. The airless tyres on the van were bought on the dark web as they were not available to the general public. They were still being experimented on. They have certainly paid dividends and are highly recommended for similar jobs.

The two police officers guarding the Rhodes residence were kidnaped, but unharmed. They were left handcuffed in an abandoned vehicle near a popular nature reserve where they were discovered by dog walkers the next morning. Just feeling cold, but healthy.

OLLIE SAVAGE

Once Ollie and Lynx got back to Ollie Savage, the police van was transformed back to its standard camper van look. The precious cargo was unloaded, and the individual items were photographed and stored, ready to go on the auction site once the news headlines hit.

The bidders will have to fight it out. Once the auction is over, the individual items will be packaged by Ollie and Lynx's special delivery service, ready for shipping to their new owners. As a gesture of good will, Ollie has offered Wizzy a fulltime job once he has successfully finished his studies.

CHAPTER TWENTY

Since getting his British citizenship, Ollie has been able to visit the country he loves so much. The British passport protects him from the Zambanian officials when he visits his family back home. He feels he owes them that. In him, they feel they have a brother, an uncle, a nephew who lives in England who can lift them out of poverty.

No one calls him by his first name anymore, just English. Since introducing his women and children to them, he wants to continue rebuilding connections with everyone for the sake of his children, the way he remembers it from his own childhood. He knows it will take time, as everyone has their own little circles now.

He still visits year on year, bringing everyone gifts, even the dead. He buys them tombstones, repairs their graves and gifts them some fresh flowers every time. Life in Zambani isn't what it used to be any more, since the passing of both his parents.

It's more of a chore that someone has to do. His mother was the last one to go. She had fought a long battle, in which she died his hero. The little old lady was 87 when she died, outliving his father. On her journey to becoming an eighteen-time great grandmother, she had conceived over twelve children, of which eight made it into adulthood. She had three miscarriages and two stills. From her own account, it was all due to poor sanitation, but word has it, she took some enormous beating back in her day.

In the end, she had gotten tired, but she did not give up that easily. Ollie could only send money and await updates from his sisters who were looking after her until she took a turn for the worst. Most of her illness had been cared for at home, she had doctors coming to her for blood work and IV therapy. In her final stretch, she was in hospital for just under a week.

By then, the girls couldn't bear with it, seeing her in that much pain. They'd call him crying, talking about how painful it was to watch her in that state. At one point, her tongue was so dry the nurses had to apply Vaseline to soften it. She died of a heart attack in the end, credit to the good heart God had given her.

Since the passing of his mother, he feels there are no family bonds anymore. It's been each to their own unless when people want money. He is just a cash machine now, people only come to him for money. The nieces and nephews he helped to raise and paid school fees for, have mostly been married and have children of their own.

Only the ones that are doing badly have stayed in touch, sending their "Hi Uncle," towards the end of the month, priming him for the kill shot. He knows it's a scam, but being the kind uncle that he is, he plays into it.

After Deena's first visit to Zambani, she met with Bonny's mother and made good friends with her. Their friendship has grown over the past two years and through that friendship, Deena was granted permission to adopt Bonny by his mother. She is now in the process of applying for his visa.

She is so excited about finally having her own son since her last pregnancy yielded a third girl. In preparation for this move, Bonny has been reading novels and taking an English-speaking course at Tampo College in Chekwa. His English has improved, significantly, through reading some of Uncle Caster's old novels too.

Ollie and Lynx have since added to their growing list of assets, land they bought in Cheshire. They are now in the process of securing investors and a construction company to assign the contract to. Construction should start as soon as they are granted permits to build three and four-bed detached houses for sale.

They both still have their day jobs for keeping up appearances, but their real work comes from Lynx's connections at Cunnings Banking. The rich folk he works for are more than happy to brag about their assets when they are out golfing or on their yachts popping bubbly.

Linda had been quiet since she got kicked out by her sister two months ago, until now. She called Ollie and asked him to give her a lift to her appointment. She has not been feeling well, she tells him. He picks her up from her residence where she rents a room in one of Ollie's shared houses. She looks very well and healthy for a supposedly unwell person.

Ollie drops her off at the hospital and waits for her in the car while catching up with Nancy, who is giving him a hard time about going all out for other people but not for her. She needs a lot of help unpacking all her stuff into her new house. Ollie feels he has let her go on for too long and hangs up the call as he sees Linda coming back.

"Hey, how did it go?" She is quiet for a minute as she throws all her bags into the back seat and straps her seatbelt on.

"Hey, I asked you a question, how did it go in there?"

"Nothing much, it's a freaking hospital what else did you expect. Let's just get out of here, let's go home. I need some rest."

"Just checking, I mean you had been in there for a while. I got tired of waiting; I was going to leave you. You could have at least sent a text if you knew your appointment was running late.

"Keep your eyes on the road and stop with the grilling. I'm sorry I took too long; these things take time."

"These things, what are they?"

"Look, I can't tell you because I do not want you to know everything about my life. "Some things are just personal; can you respect that?"

"Seriously, we have secrets now. "This is coming from the same woman that was fucking me in her sister's bed a short while back?"

"You see, there it is. "This is the reason why I can't tell you anything, you have a way of using that against me. "Thank you for making this so easy to deal with on my own." She starts crying.

Ollie apologises and reaches over to rub her back, comforting her. She sobs and finally opens up to him.

"I am sorry, I, it's eating me up. "I am so afraid to tell you. "Can you just promise me you will not freak out?"

"Ok baby, you can tell me anything. You are literally one of my wives now, you know that right?"

"I know." She continues sobbing.

"I am sorry, I just had an abortion. "My appointment was with an abortion clinic. "I just flashed our baby down the toilet in there, I am so sorry. "I just couldn't live with it, knowing I fucked my sister's hubby and kept the baby. "I just couldn't Ollie, I am so sorry. "I know I should have at least told you first, but I was just too scared you'd talk me into keeping it, sorry baby."

"You got pregnant while on the pill?"

"I wasn't taking them regularly, they once made me fat, so I just took them on the days we had sex."

"You are the dumbest bitch I know. So, you got pregnant, with my child, you didn't tell me, and you just decided it was ok to murder my…" he does not finish his sentence. He reaches his hand towards her, unclipping her seatbelt.

He wakes up in hospital hooked up to wires and tubes, just like his twins once were. The medical team congratulate him on being alive and console him for the loss of his passenger, who they had assumed to be his wife. He is told about their car accident in which she died on the spot as she was not wearing a seatbelt when their car hit a big tree at high speed.

The pathology team will soon be releasing their findings once they have concluded cause of death. For now, he needs to help the police who have come to seek his help with their investigation.

"Hi, I am PC Keith Murdoch, and this is my colleague PC Dean Coach. "We are with the Greater Manchester Traffic Police. "How are you feeling sir?"

"Please call me Ollie, I am just pleased to be alive that's all."

"Good, I am here to follow up on your accident, we are just trying to find out how that happened. "Do you think you can help us shade some light on the accident?"

"Yes, I can."

"Good, for the record, would you start by confirming your details to us please. Starting with your name, address and date of birth please?"

"Oliver Nevanji, 33 Bournemouth Way, M2 3QZ.

"Can you confirm your car's registration and insurer please?"
He confirms.

"And your passenger's details please?
He confirms.

"Thank you Mr Nevanji. Could you please tell us what had happened, leading up to the accident?"

OLLIE SAVAGE

"I had taken my sister-in-law to the hospital. On our way back, she said she wasn't feeling too well, and asked me to pull over. I told her I would stop once I had found a safe place to stop, then she started shouting at me and grabbed the steering wheel, then it all went dark," he starts crying.

"I am so sorry for your loss, Mr Nevanji. The good news is, your blood tests have come back negative for alcohol and substances of abuse, ok. We will do our further investigations and we will be in touch with you shortly. You take care and look after yourself, ok. We wish you a speedy recovery. Bye-bye now."

Deena and Nancy arrive, and Deena is falling apart. She doesn't know whether to be angry at him for killing her sister or feel sorry for him, as he almost died along with her. Nancy holds on to his hand and starts praying for his speedy recovery, but Deena just weeps as she looks on. She is under the suspicion that her family members keep dying around him. He tries to give her his hand, but she shrugs and looks away. Ollie looks at her and starts sniffling as tears start pouring down his cheeks.

OLLIE SAVAGE

All the news sources are reporting the same headlines. "A property belonging to one of Britain's highly regarded names in history was raided in broad daylight this afternoon. The two armed police officers on guard are suspected missing. With perpetrators still at large, police are appealing for help."

OLLIE SAVAGE

The author wishes to thank you for your support in buying this book and for reaching this page. Reviews are very important to us. Please help this book rank higher so other readers can find it too by leaving your review on Amazon, your Kindle device, trustpilot.com or wherever you purchased this book from.

For social media, updates on upcoming work or for film adaptation work, please follow or contact the author directly on Instagram or Twitter: @richardmauto

THE END

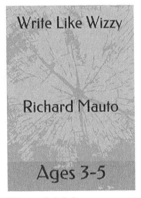

Dec 2020   Coming soon   Dec 2020

Printed in Great Britain
by Amazon